THE BLUE SAPPHIRE

By Carolyn R. Scheidies

C_R Publications

Carolyn R. Scheidies

415 E 15th
Kearney, NE 68847-6959
(308) 234-3849
crscheidies@hotmail.com Subject Line: Hope

I DEAL IN HOPE
http://IDealinHope.com

ISBN 978-0-6151-5981-2
http://www.lulu.com/content/934764

DEDICATION

The Blue Sapphire is dedicated to my sister Karin Wisdom, for all her support for my writing, for background research for this novel, and for her love for her family and God.

Thank you.

Carolyn R Scheidies

BIO

Carolyn R Scheidies is a wife, proud mother of two, and grandmother of wonderful grandchildren she loves to spoil. Though her writing career is important, it is not more important than her family or her faith. She is a member of the Hope EFC missions church in Kearney where she serves in leadership positions as well as a Sunday School teacher.

A graduate from the University of Nebraska at Kearney (UNK) with a degree in journalism, Carolyn's published credits include over two-dozen plus books, several of which have garnered awards. She's written for a variety of publications, has a regular newspaper column, worked as an editor, speaker/teacher and book reviewer. One of her Kearney Hub columns also won her an Amy Writing Award in 2013.

Through the years, Scheidies has spoken to different groups, led workshops, substitute taught in the media dept at UNK for several years and has taught adult enrichment writing classes at Central Community College. She has been interviewed on NTV, KHAS and AFR radio as well as in numerous print and online publications and had a monthly book review segment on NTV when she was a regular book reviewer. http://IDealinHope.com.

Whatever she does, Carolyn's goal is to share hope found in Jesus Christ.

Prologue

The blue-eyed nymph sitting on the corral gate
called out to her older sister. "Cynthia." Taking off her
straw cowboy hat, Jeanette wiped her forehead before
jamming it back over her long brunette hair hanging
down her back in a thick braid. "Do something else.
Hold it," she cried, jumping down from the gate. "I lost
a boot."

Hopping toward the lost footwear, the young girl
thrust her foot into the offending black cowboy boot
decorated with white swirls on the tops and pulled it on.
Dusting off her hands onto the legs of her blue jeans, she
hopped back onto the gate.

Cynthia, the tall, svelte teenager with the same
startling shade of blue eyes as her younger sister,
Jeanette, shook her head. "Jeanette Roberts, really. You
positively must grow up. Stop trying to be a cowgirl."

"I like dressing like this." Momentarily, the younger
girl's adoration waned in the face of her sister's
criticism. "I don't want to be all got up like you. But if
you don't want to act any more..." She started to hop
down.

"I'm sorry to criticize your taste, little sister. One of
these days you'll grow out of cheap jeans and cowboy
hats." Cynthia laughed. Swinging her long blond hair
over her shoulder, she struck a pose. "To be or not to

be," she intoned dramatically. With a comedic flare, she pranced about the hard-packed corral flinging out her slender arms as she quoted the passage. Her antics had her adoring sister laughing so hard she had to cling to the sturdy wooden gate to keep from falling off.

Pulling her sister from the gate, Cynthia drew her into an impromptu trot around the corral. Finally, both exhausted, they opened the gate. Cynthia breezed through, letting Jeanette close it. They collapsed onto a carpet of green lawn laughing.

Before they fully caught their breath, their kindly, rather plump mother brought out two tall glasses and a plate of cookies.

Leaping to her feet, Jeanette hurried to her aid. "Thanks, Mom. This is great, isn't it Sis." She handed her sister a frosty glass, before taking her own. Sitting down, she took the plate and set it between her sister and herself on the ground. Taking a long sip, she savored it before saying, "There's nothing like your homemade lemonade, Mom. No powder can beat this stuff."

Cynthia agreed, "Yeah, Mom, great lemonade. It sure hits the spot."

Their mother smiled. "I just thought you might be ready for a snack."

As Mrs. Roberts returned to the farmhouse, Jeanette picked up one of cookies still warm from the oven. "No one comes close to the taste of her peanut butter cookies either."

Rolling onto her stomach, Cynthia bit into one of the soft rounds. "Umm. Give me another."

Overhead, the summer sun beamed down warm and bright on the two girls. Insects whizzed back and forth, and more than once Jeanette waved away a fly. Cynthia grimaced. "I hate all these bugs. Someday, I'm going to live in a city where I never have to bother with all these bugs." She squealed as she brushed off an ant persistently crawling up her leg.

"I like living in the country." Shielding her eyes, Jeanette surveyed the farm around her from the large farmhouse to the green pasture land to the fields where corn and milo waved back and forth in the light breeze.

"Breathe in that fresh air. I'm glad I live here close to the earth. Makes one feel close to God." She hugged her knees.

"I don't like it," her sister declared. "I hate dirt. I hate living in this forsaken place. Who's ever heard of Kansas anyway?"

"Dorothy."

Her sister stared. "Who?"

"Dorothy. You know, from the Wizard of Oz."

"Fairy tales," her sister said with a sigh of long-suffering. "Just fairy tales. Jeanette, for all your practicality in some matters, your head is in the clouds. Life is what you make it or what you take from it. No tornado is going to whisk you off to your enchanted land or to prince charming."

Again she sighed. "You've been so sheltered."

"And you haven't been." Jeanette's anger rose. "Because, I like the country and being good, doesn't mean I don't live in the real world."

Her sister only shook her head. "I can't wait to get out of this place. I want to be surrounded by beautiful people, rich, beautiful people."

"Kansas can boast of a number of Miss Americas," Jeanette reminded her. "The state is known for its beautiful women." Surveying her sister, she commented, "Maybe you should try out. You'd make a great Miss America."

Her sister tilted her head thoughtfully. "Maybe, but it takes so long. Some girls try year after year and never get to the pageant. Still..."

"Sure, why not try?" Jeanette hated to see her sister unhappy. "The winners get all kinds of scholarships and things."

"I don't want to go to college."

"What! You can't mean that, Cynthia. Why Mom and Dad plan on both of us going to college?" She frowned, "What else would you do?"

Shrugging, Cynthia surveyed her sister. "Get married maybe."

"You're too young. Besides, I thought you said you wanted to get away from Kansas."

Cynthia snorted. "Who said I had to marry one of the local yokels?"

Jeanette winced. Sometimes her sister could be cruel. "What about Bob? I thought you liked him."

"Not enough to marry him." Getting up, she spun around. Throwing out her arms, she cried, "I want to be free, free to do what I want. I want to taste life to its fullest. I want to do what I want when I want."

"But Cynthia, aren't you interested in God's plan for your life?"

Stopping abruptly, Cynthia stared down at her sister through narrowed eyes. "This will shock you, my oh-so-saintly sister, but no...I don't much care about God's plan, unless it matches my own plan."

Jeanette's mouth dropped open. "Cynthia...."

Her sister flopped back down beside her. "Oh, don't worry. I don't plan on doing anything so dreadful. I just want to be an actress, a famous actress, with more money than I know what to do with. You'll be proud then of your wild sister, and so will Mom and Dad."

"But," Jeanette protested, "we're proud of you now. Please don't do anything foolish Cynthia, something you'll regret."

Her sister grimaced. "Why not? The folks have you, the perfect little sister who never does anything wrong. They don't need me. Mark my words, Sis, one day you'll have a choice to make as well as I. Then what will you do? What then?"

CHAPTER ONE:

Absently Jeanette rubbed the telltale band where her engagement ring had so recently circled her finger. For so long she wore that ring. It now seemed incredible she permitted the engagement to continue for so long. Jeanette blinked away the tears stinging her large blue eyes. Sniffing, she tucked a stray lock behind her ear.

In her hand, she held the letter, carefully written, and so serious. How different the tone of the letter from this older John than from the John she first met, ages ago...or so it seemed. And Brad. What about Brad, her fiancé--or who was her fiancé? What did she owe him after all this time? Her own indecision and stubbornness haunted her.

She shook the brunette hair that fell just below her earlobe, liking the feel of its longer length after wearing it short for the last couple of years. How she tried to please, tried to remake who she was into something Brad could be proud to call his. She shuttered at the thought of being owned by anyone. But that was almost what she allowed herself to be--owned, like a sports car or vacation condo.

Again she shook her head. All her planning, all her determination, all the things she had so carefully tucked away burst forth, and why? The letter. It crinkled now in her hand. How could such a simple thing as a piece of paper precipitate such a disaster, if disaster it was. And if it was, why did she feel such a sense of release?

Shuddering, she recalled how Brad exploded when she mentioned the letter from John, more from hurt, she understood now, than anger. Had it been building up within him as well as her, the hurt, the questions, the anger?

Frowning, Jeanette ran trembling fingers through her hair, causing the sun to catch auburn highlights in its rich depth. Brad liked her hair short. John, on the other hand, liked the way her hair flowed over her shoulders and down her back. Fingering the softly curved ends, Jeanette wished she had never cut it, but then, if she had not tried to please Brad by cutting it, she would never have realized how much she liked the longer style, or the girl she used to be--young, naive, believing fairy tales came true. They didn't. She knew that now; had known for sometime. Even a fairy princess had choices, but it was all so much easier in stories. Too bad she refused to admit her fairy tale world was just that, a fairy tale. Reality was a harsh master, but she was learning.

Fairy tales. Brad never did like her romantic turn of mind, but then there was so much the tall, successful Brad disliked about her. He tried to change the country goose into a sophisticated swan. He failed. How Cynthia would have laughed at the dilemma in which Cynthia's younger sister found herself and by her own stubborn choices. But she cared for Brad, hadn't she? How hard, she tried to please him. Tried so hard.

Jeanette gulped back tears. From gently sharing her faith, she became a zealot. Finally, to please him, she even stopped, as he put it, badgering him about a 'personal' relationship with Jesus Christ.

She tried so hard, prayed so hard for things to be right again. After all, she had agreed to marry Brad. Even now, she felt a sense of disquiet at the scene between them. And, all because of the letter that arrived on the eve of her wedding to one of the most eligible bachelors in the community. She could hear the comments, and the gossip.

Shuddering, she reviewed in her mind what she would say to her folks. And she would have to tell them, alone. "Oh, Lord. How could I have gone so wrong? I failed you. I failed in my commitment to Brad, and, I failed Mom and Dad--and after all they did for me. I failed, and yet... Slowly, she walked toward the footbridge and her rendezvous with her past.

Fleetingly, she thought of her sister and gulped back tears as she thought back to the girl she used to be not so long past.

***

By her senior year of high school, Jeanette had her life pretty well planned out for herself. She set aside four years of college to get a teaching degree. Though, unlike her sister, she loved the outdoors, she also loved to sew. Even now, she fondly recalled the day her patient mother taught an energetic six-year-old how to make a straight stitch. In an afternoon, she learned to sew simple doll clothes and was hooked on sewing.

Under her mother's tutelage and through her participation in 4-H, she soon learned to weld the sewing machine and, by the time she was ten, could whip out any number of items. By the time she turned thirteen, she proudly wore her own creations in shirts and skirts and dresses, though she still preferred T-shirts and jeans.

Cooking, if anything, was an even greater outlet for her creativity. When Jeanette was but fourteen, her mother left the baking of breads and desserts in her competent hands.

Jeanette did much more than bake and sew. Under her skillful hands, bread became a creation, and her clothes were design originals admired by all her friends. She won so many awards at both county and state fairs, her father put up a giant cork board on her wall on which she carefully pinned her numerous ribbons.

As she grew older, she found herself helping younger children with their projects. The idea grew that she would like to make her life's work teaching. She loved the idea of sharing her knowledge with those younger than herself, and she picked out ProMark as her college of choice.

Unlike her sister, she had little desire to move far from her roots. And she didn't need to. Not only did the four year college have a solid Family and Consumer Science degree she wanted to pursue, along with an art minor, but her aunt and uncle lived in the mid-sized

Kansas town. She felt a certain comfort in knowing family would be close.

She knew her parents saved since her birth for the time she would go to college. How they had all worked to make a go of the windswept farm, all except her older sister Cynthia. For a moment, Jeanette's lips turned down. Cynthia! With a groan, she forced herself to think of her scholarship to college and the job she had waiting McFadden. Yes, this little Kansas girl was all set to storm the doors of higher learning.

In a moment of time it all came to a screeching halt.

Happily planning for college, Jeanette returned from a shopping trip with her best friend Sandie. Laughing, the two girls dragged their purchases into the large comfortable two-story farm house.

"Mother," Jeanette called, slipping into the door. "Mother, want to see what we bought?" Setting down her bags and boxes on the counter, she called out again, "Sandie's staying for dinner, all right?"

The silence of the house sent chills up her back.

"Do you think she drove into town?" her friend asked as she came back from the bedroom where she'd put more of Jeanette's things.

"She never said anything. Maybe she needed to help Dad out in the field." For all that, Jeanette felt a sense of disquiet. "A note. If she left, there'd be a note."

They searched, but found nothing. Shrugging to ease the tension, Jeanette picked up her bags. "At least we can put these away." As she pulled a bag off the counter, a piece of paper fluttered to the floor.

Stooping, Sandie picked it up. "Here it is." She blanched as she handed it to Jeanette. "Oh, Jeanette. Read it."

At the tremor in the voice of her friend, she grabbed the paper.

"Jeanette," it read, "your father's had an accident."

"Oh, Sandie, the tractor upended on top of father. Oh, no! Sandie, I have to get to the hospital--now!"

"Come on, I'll drive."

Jeanette remembered the joy in hearing her father was not going to die and the frustration for all of them when the weeks passed with little change in his condition. Recovery was more than slow; it was frustratingly, agonizingly, almost non existent. She recalled her anger at her sister's light-hearted attitude about the whole thing.

Since leaving the farm life she detested, Cynthia seldom returned home. They heard little enough about her or the man she ran off to marry. Her letters were little more than hurried notes that said little. Not once did she inquire about financial arrangements or offer to help out.

Vividly, Jeanette recalled the disintegration of her own plans as the doctor told them, "I'm sorry, but the leg is not healing properly. The hip has been crushed. I suggest you see an orthopedist about a joint replacement."

Her blue eyes dark with fear, her mother whispered, "Will, will he be all right?"

"He will live. His ribs are healing nicely and his concussion is not serious, but that hip is bad. Something has to be done about that. I can give you the name of a doctor in Salina."

"Thank you, Doctor," her mother managed.

Later, Jeanette approached her mother. "Mom, I've been thinking." She hesitated. "The insurance isn't covering all this, is it?"

"No, dear, but God will see us through." As she did when Jeanette was a child, Mrs. Roberts smoothed her daughter's fly away hair away from her face. "It might be tight for a while, but it will be all right."

"About the farm? I know the neighbors have been great and all, but they have their own farms to tend. What will we do for income?"

Her mother's shoulders slumped. "I don't know."

"I'd like to postpone college and help on the farm. Not only could I work the farm, but it would save money. We can use the money from my college fund."

Her mother's shoulders snapped back. "No. We'll make do without that. Your father and I will not take away your chance to go to college. There has to be another way."

More than once Jeanette offered to postpone her college, but her mother would have none of it, not until it became apparent the surgery was not solving the problem as they all hoped and prayed.

That summer, her sister returned once again. While the rest of the family stared, she greeted them as though she'd been away on a shopping trip. Laughing, she ran up the stairs. "You don't mind if I stay the week or two, do you?"

"I suppose not." Mrs. Roberts seemed almost relieved to have her older daughter at home.

Jeanette began, "But Mother…?"

"Dear, let's just be glad our prodigal is at home for now and we know she's safe."

Jeanette pursed her lips. She felt only frustration and bitterness she hid behind a brittle smile. "Where's your husband, Cynthia?"

"Gone."

Her mother swung around. "What do you mean gone?"

Cynthia waved her hand carelessly. "We were tired of each other, so we split."

Mrs. Roberts tensed. "You are working things out, right?"

"Why bother? No, Mother we aren't. We're divorced."

The proverbial pin could have been heard dropping in the silence. Mrs. Roberts appeared to be choking. Jeanette clenched her teeth as she put an arm about her mother. "Are you all right, Mom?"

"Oh, Cynthia," Mrs. Roberts finally managed. "I'm sorry, so sorry." Cynthia turned away with a shrug, giving Jeanette the impression she didn't care, not one bit.

Much to Jeanette's frustration, the irresponsible Cynthia breezed in and out of their lives for several months. Thoughts of the sister Jeanette once idolized now brought only a churning to Jeanette's middle.

Cynthia didn't bring home her latest "friend," knowing how her parents felt about her lifestyle, but she never failed to regaled her little sister with her exploits.

"Why don't you stay and help out?" Jeanette demanded, tired of her sister's irresponsibility and resentful of always being, as Cynthia termed it, "the dependable one."

Cynthia's musical laughter grated, "Surely you cannot expect me to tend father." She inspected her brightly polished nails, "And I will absolutely not do chores...not like you, Sis. That's not for me."

"Look around you, Cynthia. We could use your help. Father is barely getting around, much less able to do chores. The neighbors help, but most is left up to Mom and me."

"I wasn't cut out to be a common farm laborer," Cynthia said quietly, "and neither were you."

"You could help around the house at least."

Sighing, Cynthia reached out to touch her sister's cheek. Jeanette pulled away. "What you're doing hurts Mom and Dad. Don't you care?"

Pain flitted across the older girl's face. "Of course I care," she retorted, "but this is my life, and I must live it my way. Can't you see that?"

Jeanette bit her lips to keep herself from saying, "And a fine mess you've made of it, too." From the look

on her sister's face, Cynthia well knew what she thought.

"Look Jeanette. I know you're doing all you can to save this farm, but wouldn't it be better for everyone if you just sell it and move to town? Then you could go to college like you've always planned."

"Oh, Cynthia, you don't understand. Dad is a farmer."

Mrs. Roberts, too, tried to talk to her elder daughter. Jeanette resented the tight lips of her mother when Cynthia dismissed any attempt to talk to her seriously; resented the pain Cynthia caused both her parents. Even when she was still in grade school, Jeanette remembered some of the violent confrontations her parents had with her sister over her friends, her late nights, and her refusal to comply with their wishes to get involved with church. Right out of high school, she eloped with a young man of whom they did not approve.

To this day, Jeanette vividly recalled that night. Only a few clouds shielded the bright silvery moon. Once more, Cynthia was late coming home from her date with the handsome Dan. Older than most of the boys she dated, Dan, moved into the area from the west coast. He had a dash which drew Cynthia like a magnet.

Jeanette worried about Cynthia who grew more belligerent with each date. Always it was Dan this and Dan that. His folks also took to her.

When her sister didn't come home, Mr. Roberts discreetly begin calling her friends. No one had seen her

or Dan. Haggard from lack of sleep, Mr. Roberts, along
with his wife and Jeanette, decided to call the sheriff
when Cynthia and Dan pulled up in front of the
farmhouse. Her face radiant, Cynthia announced,
"We're married."

They saw little of her after that, for she soon moved
away with her husband and his family. Sporadically,
they heard about her life, and what they heard pained
them. Still, after five years when Cynthia came home
with the news of her divorce, they were devastated.

"Divorce?" Her mother could scarcely say the word,
yet Jeanette knew her parents weren't about to let the
subject pass by without trying to deal with it--however
painful. "Dear, there has never been a divorce in our
family."

Cynthia tossed her head carelessly, "Well then, I'm
the first. I know how you worship commitment, but not
every relationship works out, Mother."

"Did he abuse you, Cynthia?" her father asked with a
growl. "See other women?"

"Really, father. Not everyone gets a divorce because
of abuse, and no, he wasn't seeing anyone else. No, I
would never stand for such a thing. I just got tired of
him. He couldn't hold a job and frankly, I was tired of
living with his parents. Then I met Jeremy." Her eyes
softened. "He is handsome and rich and ...."

Jeanette asked, "Are you're getting married again?"

"Married! I tried that, Sis. No way. Not again." For a
moment, just a moment, Jeanette thought she saw pain

and disillusionment in her sister's eyes. "Wait until you meet Jeremy."

Always polite, Jeanette's mother offered. "I'll make up the guest room for him. How long will he be staying?"

Cynthia laughed then, derisively, "No need Mom, Jeremy and I, we...."

Her father's frown stopped her. "Young lady. If you're about to suggest what I think you are, forget it. There will not be such goings on in this house. When your mother and I built this house, we asked the Lord to bless it. Your friend will have to stay elsewhere." His voice hardened. "You made a commitment Cynthia, and you better consider returning to your husband and making a go of it. We'll help by providing counseling with a minister..."

Glaring at them, Cynthia shrilled. "I'm sick and tired of your old fashioned morality. Get real. This isn't the stone age."

"Cynthia!" her father bellowed in a manner that always made Jeanette shiver. Her easy going father seldom lost his temper and did only with great provocation. "We brought you up to know the Lord, and, however much we love you, we cannot force you to live as we would like you to live. But we do have a say in how you behave in our home."

"Father! Mother?" Cynthia shrugged, "Well, if that's the way it's going to be."

"It is." Her father stood his ground, but Jeanette saw the raw pain in his eyes as his first born stomped from the house. They hadn't heard from her for another year.

Jeanette promised herself she would never disappoint her parents as her sister had done. Maybe that is why she had not minded overmuch, at least so she told herself, when she gave up her plans to attend ProMark to stay home and help on the farm. The trust money was gone anyway. It went to pay hospital and doctor bills.

With the help of her high school art teacher, she won a scholarship to Colby Community college where she attended for a year and a half. For her sake as well as her father's, she prayed her father would once more get well enough to work the farm he loved so much.

She certainly could have done without Cynthia's mocking comments about her "sacrifice" as though she was not only naive, but stupid. Someday, she would show her, someday. It did pay to follow the right path, it did!

Stubbornly, she determined she would never be rebellious like Cynthia or flit from man to man. Regardless of how Cynthia bragged, Jeanette saw a deep hopelessness in her sister's eyes, but Cynthia would not let Jeanette help her. No, Cynthia's way was not her way, not God's way. One day Jeanette would find the one man God had for her and stay beside him the rest of her life.

Jeanette lifted her head and stared out over the stream bubbling merrily under the bridge as it meandered through the park, green with new growth. Its cool clear waters soothed her bruised spirit. No longer would she run from her problems or her inner conflicts. It had taken her long enough to face the truth and whatever this meeting brought she would handle--with God's help.

From somewhere in back of her she heard the happy cries of laughter from children playing on the slides and swings. Heard the whirl of the merry-go-round. It had been so long since she laughed in such an carefree fashion.

Had she been all that much better than Cynthia? Tears started again, and she wiped them away. At least her sister had been honest in her rejection of her Lord.

Jeanette shoulders bowed under her burden, even while a strange sense of resiliency filled her. She had failed. Yet God was still there. Raising her head, Jeanette straightened her shoulders. First she would see John and apologize for the hurt she caused him. Then, she would go home.

Squeezing her eyes shut, Jeanette clutched the small ornate box in her pocket that symbolized her greatest failure of all--the blue sapphire.

Where had she gone wrong? Had it all started even before she left for college; started in her desire to be as different from Cynthia as possible?

Closing her eyes she saw herself as she was then, studying her worn Bible.

CHAPTER TWO:

"And we know that all things work together for good
to them that love God, to them who are the called
according to his purpose." Taking up her pen, Jeanette
carefully underlined the verse in Romans before closing
her well-worn Bible and setting it on the stand beside
the bed.

She could have purchased a new Bible in a new
version, but something of her romantic heart moved to
the music and lilt of the ancient English of her old King
James Bible. However worn, she found it hard to part
with the Bible she had earned by memorizing 100 verses
in her Sunday School class when she was nine.

Now she sought comfort and direction as she
dropped to her knees beside the sagging mattress of her
single bed. There was no carpeting on the wood floors,
and she was grateful for the cushioning of the large rag
rug woven for her by her mother for her 12th birthday.
Smoothing the patchwork quilt on the bed, she thought
about all the painstaking stitches it took to put it
together.

She thought with gratitude about her mother's
patience as she showed her young daughter how to cut
pieces of old material into blocks and sew them into a
pleasing pattern. She recalled how her mother helped her

back the cover and quilt it all by hand. Every stitch showed her mother's love and her own determination. At least with the quilt she knew exactly what she was supposed to do, but life, her life pattern wasn't so simple.

"Lord, what do you want me to do? I want to continue my education, and I've gone as far as I can here. But can I leave the farm now? Dad is getting better, but the doctor says he'll never be as strong or as agile as he was before." Her prayer continued for sometime as she debated her situation with her Heavenly Father.

Debate was the key, for she did more than ask direction and wait. Jeanette argued the merits of staying or of doing what Uncle Silas suggested she do. Well, more than suggested.

"My dear, you've buried yourself here on the farm long enough." Uncle Silas said as they walked around the yard of the large white farmhouse that needed a coat of paint, but was otherwise well kept up. Though both taller and wider than her wiry father, Silas wore one of her dad's windbreakers against the chill of the fall. "It's time for you to go on to ProMark."

"But Uncle Silas, father..."

"Your father, my brother, is getting around better than any of his doctors thought he ever would again."

"But it's still so difficult for him." Jeanette blinked back tears. She hated to see her father struggle with chores that once came so easily to him. Though not large, he'd made up for it with determination, boundless energy and strength.

"True, but he does not need babying by the misconstrued help of his dutiful daughter," Silas told her firmly.

Jeanette's eyes flashed, but she held in her anger at the unjust accusation. "Uncle Silas, Dad still needs me. You know he can't do all the chores himself. Mom can't do everything else."

"That's true, but it's time for you to start living your own life."

"I'm perfectly happy here, really I am," Jeanette said, but her protestations sounded weak even to her. "What other options are there? I won't let them sell the farm like Cynthia suggested."

"I quite agree. That would not be best for your father, but neither is it good for you to pour your life into this place." He held up a hand to forestall any further protest. "Hear me out, Jeanette. I care about my brother, but I care about my niece as well." He patted her arm. "So, at my suggestion, I might add, your father is planning to hire someone to help him with the more difficult chores. Both he and your mother agree it is time for you to continue your education."

"Hire someone! Dad can't afford..."

"Jeanette," she heard exasperation in his tone, "farming is a gamble at best. With your help, and lots of prayer, this place has stayed afloat. Markets are pretty steady right now, and thanks to you and your mother, there is no debt outstanding on the farm." When Jeanette would have interrupted, Silas wrapped an arm about her shoulder. "Further, the doctor bills are getting paid on a regular basis."

"But there are still bills. And you forget, my college money went to pay off some of those bills." From the look on the face of her uncle, Jeanette knew Silas heard the note of sadness, the loss of a dream.

"I am well aware of that, Jeanette, but there are scholarships available. And, I have a job waiting for you at my store in McFadden."

Silent a moment, Jeanette said quietly, "Uncle Silas, you're a dear, but even with help, how would I possibly pay for room and board? No, I must stop dreaming and accept where I am at right now. I guess Cynthia was right in saying I've been sheltered. I have been in so many ways. Somehow, I thought everything would work out if we just kept trying, but they haven't." Sucking in a deep breath, she straightened her shoulders. "I'll find a job in town to help pay off the bills."

"Doing what? Slinging hash in some greasy fast-food place?"

"There's nothing wrong with being a waitress. It's a perfectly respectable job. And it is something I could do."

"Yes, it is, but is that what you want to do for the rest of your life?"

"Of course not. Once we get the bills paid off and Dad on his feet, I'll save for college."

"How long will that take. Are you planning to put off marriage and family?"

Jeanette blushed, "Uncle Silas, I haven't even met anyone I'd like to marry yet."

"That's my point. How will you find that special someone here? I'd guess most of your classmates have already paired off or left the area."

Jeanette thought of her friend Sandie, engaged and soon to marry her childhood sweetheart. Something inside ached for the happiness of her friend, the sureness of her relationship. "God will bring the right person into my life."

"Yes, we must not limit God. If you can trust him for your life's mate, why not trust Him to take care of your folks and the financial needs?" He didn't let her interrupt.

"God has given you special talents. Doesn't He ask us to develop and use all the talents He's given us?"

"Of course, Uncle. I'll always cook and sew. Surely, there is a way to use those gifts for Him right here. Besides, there is still the matter of money. How do you suppose God will supply. Money doesn't grow on trees."

Silas put a hand on her arm. "Jeanette, you know how much your aunt Evelyn and I love young people, but our own five are all grown and gone from home." He chuckled, "Gone for sure. Our marines, Randy and Jim, always get sent to the latest hot spots. Janice and her husband pastor in Texas, and you know our youngest Reece and his wife recently left to plant a church in Romania. It isn't as though our brood can drop in on weekends. We want you to come live with us while you go to school."

Hope dawned on her face. "Oh, but, Uncle Silas, I couldn't impose like that. I won't be a burden on Aunt Evelyn, not after the stroke she had two years ago."

Silas chuckled. "That's one of the reasons I want you with us. I thought, maybe, you could help out a bit with household chores and the cooking."

This time Jeanette laughed. "Like maybe my pecan pie you're always raving over."

Silas' eyes twinkled. "Something like that. Well, how about it?"

"How about it?" Jeanette felt excitement simmer inside. "Do you think it will work?"

"Are you ready to try?" Silas searched her face, nodded as though satisfied with what he saw.

Grinning, Jeanette nodded. "As long as Mom and Dad are sure...."

Silas steered her back toward the house. "Come on, let's see what they say."

"Of course, we'll be fine," her parents told her, and she could see they really did want this for her. Even God's Word spoke to her, "all things work together for good."

When she got up from her knees, Jeanette knew what she would do. If she applied for scholarships and got them, she'd go. Already the middle of the fall semester, it was unlikely she'd be able to get anything at this late date, at least not so as to start after the New Year. But she sent in applications anyway and left the rest up to God.

Actually, she figured there was no way she'd get in next semester. As much as the prospect pleased her to go on with her studies and to live with her favorite aunt and uncle, she really doubted it could happen--at least not until the next fall. Putting the whole thing to the back of her mind, she launched into the holiday season.

Now that her father was finally on the mend, she and her mother decorated the house in celebration while he watched. Red ribbons and evergreen branches looped over the door frame moldings and candles lit the large living room window. Carols echoed softly through the house.

The next day, with her father beside her in the car, she drove to town to find the perfect tree. At the third place they looked they found it, a nine-foot tree loaded with green branches.

Back home, it took all three of them to drag it into the living room and settle it into a sturdy tree stand her father made several years previous. As the afternoon flowed into evening, Jeanette popped popcorn and set the bowl beside her father in his easy chair.

Opening the box of ornaments her mother brought down from the attic earlier in the day, Jeanette began to sort out the many Christmas bells, fragile balls and assorted ornaments she and Cynthia made and brought home over the years. Between them, she and her mother managed to string the multicolored lights before adding

the ornaments. An angel topped the tree. Underneath, her mother smoothed the bright red skirt Jeanette made one Christmas as a gift.

Getting up, her father took out the manger scene and carefully set it out on the mantle among the greenery over the old fireplace that crackled with warmth, especially if one got too close. The Nativity scene had been part of Jeanette's Christmas since she'd been born and made her feel the warmth and security of her loving home.

"All right," said her father, "it's time." He snapped off the light switch, leaving the room in the glow from the fireplace and soft lights of the tree. "We have a lot to be thankful for," he choked. Putting one arm about his wife and the other around his daughter, he began to sing, "Joy to the world, the Lord has come." Reverently, they joined in.

Yes, there was much to be thankful for, Jeanette thought. Surely, she could not expect more. She was wrong.

Two days before Christmas, a letter arrived in the mail from ProMark. Opening it with trembling fingers, Jeanette read the letter, then again. With a whoop, she ran from her blue and white bedroom to the kitchen where her mother fixed supper.

"Mom, look. I don't believe it. I got it! I got a scholarship. Two actually, and it will pay for nearly, let's see, nearly two-thirds of my tuition. That leaves mostly books and other supplies to pay for. Can we do it? Can we?"

The bright hope faded from her eyes. "Even with my job, it will still cost a lot of money. Maybe I should just forget it, and stay home."

Frowning, her mother grabbed her shoulders none too gently. "That's enough, Jeanette. We prayed about this. It was agreed that should you receive a scholarship, you would go. This is God's answer. And you will, you are going.

"Jeanette, remember God, not you, and certainly not me, is in control. Trust Him."

"Trust in the Lord with all your heart; and lean not unto your own understanding." The verse learned to help earn her Bible, rolled off Jeanette's tongue.

Her mother continued, "'In all your ways acknowledge him, and he shall direct your paths.' Now if you don't forget that, my dear, you will be just fine. I only wish..."

She did not need to say anything more, as both their minds turned to Cynthia.

Cynthia breezed in the day before Christmas. As usual, she had given no warning of her visit. But, despite the grief she continued to cause them, Mr. & Mrs. Roberts welcomed their daughter with open arms. Jeanette knew they hoped that this time Cynthia had come home, not only to them, but to her Heavenly Father. Jeanette felt only impatience with her irresponsible sister and tired of her antics.

For the sake of her parents, Jeanette, too, hoped Cynthia had changed, but was not surprised she hadn't.

In fact, Cynthia was more excited than she had been for a long time.

Whirling about the large comfortable living room with its heavy rust-colored furnishings and matching curtains Jeanette and her mother designed and sewed the summer before, Cynthia told them. "You'll never believe what happened! I tried out for this commercial-- and I got it! I made it. I'm an actress." She laughed at the surprise on the faces of her family.

Her mother recovered first. "Why that's wonderful, Cynthia? You've always wanted to be an actress."

Jeanette spoke up, "And you were wonderful in all those school plays."

Cynthia laughed, "Oh, Sis, you were too little to remember much of that."

"I was old enough to know you were the most talented person on stage," Jeanette said, her lips set in a stubborn twist. "Besides, you performed for me all the time." She thought of the impromptu performances in the corral.

"Always loyal, aren't you, little Sis." For a moment Cynthia grew serious. "Don't ever change that Sis."

Her excitement returned, and she regaled her family with a dramatized version of her search for work that kept them laughing until she finished. For a short while, tension disappeared under their genuine happiness for Cynthia.

However, tension quickly returned when her folks began to ask a few more questions about her life.

Especially about her tendency to, as she put it, "get out of another contract to be able to do the commercial."

Jeanette could see they did not mean to pry, but Cynthia withdrew into haughty silence. The rest of her time with them, everyone made a point not to probe too deeply. But after Cynthia left, Jeanette found her father in his study with tears in his eyes.

"Father?"

"Oh, Jeanette, your sister is so mixed up. She's destroying her life and doesn't seem to realize it, and she won't let us help her."

Jeanette knelt at his feet and stared up into his face. "Father, we're praying for her. She'll come back to the Lord. I know she will."

Laying a hand, rough from hard labor, on her shoulder he asked. "And you, Jeanette. Will you stand strong for the Lord? Will you keep your commitment to Him? To others?"

She could not bear his hurt. "Father, I will. I will keep my commitments. I promise."

She could also not hurt them by refusing to go to ProMark when she realized they really wanted her to go. With the letter in her hands and her mother's firm support, her dreams suddenly took wing. She was going on to college.

Excitement flowed through her as she packed for her trip to McFadden after the holidays. With loving hands, she folded the skirt and sweater set her parents had given her for Christmas. Her gaze caught the warm coat they had also given her and her eyes teared. They had given her so much more than material gifts.

Well, she would make them proud of her. She could see herself on that platform in a couple of years. Yes, she planned on finishing her courses in record time. The less time it took for her to complete her schooling, the less burden she'd be on her family. She'd get a job sharing her knowledge with eager young people and use part of her income to help her family.

She could see the proud look on the faces of her mother and father, neither of which had been able to go on to school.

Uncle Silas told her, "Your father wanted to go on to seminary, but when our father died in his senior year, he felt he had to stay home and make a go of the farm for our sakes. He never left, and he grew to love farming. But, he does not want that for you; not when he feels God has something else for you. Listen to him, Jeanette. Your father is a very wise man."

Her friend Sandie Marcuson offered to drive her to McFadden, an offer Jeanette eagerly accepted. Other than the battered farm truck, the Roberts had only one family car and no money for another. All Jeanette had for transportation was her old bike her father helped her tie onto the car. Snow crunched underfoot as they loaded the back seat and trunk with Jeanette's belongings.

On one hand, Jeanette wished for her own car. On the other hand, she was glad to have this time with her best friend. "I'll miss you Sandie." Jeanette told her red-haired friend. "Ever since you moved into the area when

we were high school freshmen, we've seen each other at
least once a week."

Sandie added, "And talked on the phone for hours."
They both laughed.

"I don't know if my schedule—or yours--will stand
for much long distance calling. And it isn't as though I
have a fancy smart phone either." She held up a flip
phone. "It a pay-as-you phone."

Sandie told her, "There's always e-mail."

"I'll need access," Jeanette told her, "but we'll see.
Even if Uncle Silas doesn't have internet at home—and I
do not know that for sure, of course the school does.
Still, I will miss being around as you and Jeff make the
wedding plans."

"I know. But soon you'll be busy with school and
new friends." She winked. "Just don't forget your old
friends."

"I'd never do that!"

Sighing, Sandie glanced over at her friend. "Jeanette,
I'm going to tell you something that I hope you take the
right way. Lighten up. Since your father's accident
you've gotten so serious about everything. Take time to
laugh. Even the Bible says, 'a merry heart does good
like a medicine.'"

Jeanette turned to stare out the window at the rolling
Kansas prairies that rippled in winter wheat. Her friend
did not understand. Sandie's family was well off and
had never had to worry about money. She was engaged
to Jeff, a wonderful Christian young man. Besides, she
didn't know about Cynthia, not much anyway. By the

time Sandie and her family moved to town, Cynthia was old news, and the family seldom spoke much about her outside the confines of their own family.

"Jeanette. You're a million miles away. Jeanette, you mad at me or something?"

Forcing a smile, Jeanette glanced over at her friend. "No, of course not. Just thinking. Maybe you're right about me being too serious."

"Well, I'm making progress--you heard me. Ready to lighten up?"

Jeanette grinned. "How about stopping and letting me treat you to ice cream."

"That certainly won't lighten me up," Sandie groaned, patting her slender hips.

Surveying her friend's figure, Jeanette commented dryly, "It my treat. Besides, you haven't a thing to worry about."

The girls grinned at one another. "All right let's do it."

At Salina they pulled off interstate 70 to look for a place to eat.

Jeanette pointed to the left. "Hey, that looks good."

Sandie grinned at the sight of the large ice cream sundae sign over the door. "Looks good to me, too."

Five minutes later, they parked the two-toned burgundy car and walked inside to order. Ice cream in hand, they found a table, sat down to eat and continue reminiscing. Their laughter reached a nearby table, causing a young man to glance toward their table.

Catching his frankly admiring glaze, Jeanette blushed bright pink, a trait she hated in herself but was unable to stop. Her attempts to halt the flush spreading across her light complexion not only made it worse, but also made her angry.

"Appears to me," Sandie whispered, "you made a conquest."

Jeanette glared at her friend. "If you think I'm interested in men who pick up women at truck stops."

"Calm down girl. He hasn't done anything but admire you," Sandie said. "Lighten up, remember?"

"This isn't what I had in mind. He makes me uncomfortable," Jeanette whispered back. Feeling his gaze, she felt her face deepen with tell-tale warmth.

How dare the rude young man stare at her! Raising her chin, Jeanette stared back, only to be caught by his infectious grin. For some reason she could not fathom, she found it echoed on her own face. Suddenly aware of the silly grin on her lips, Jeanette's cheeks flamed again, and she stared down at her sundae in embarrassment.

"Why won't he go away?" she muttered more to herself than to her friend.

Sandie dared glance his way. "Umm. Nice looking. Thick dark curly hair, strong chin, rugged, broad shoulders. I think he's tall, from the looks of those long legs."

"Oh hush, Sandie. He'll hear you."

Sandie grinned at her friend. "Well, he doesn't look like a mass murderer to me."

"You never know."

"All right, I'll stop teasing you, but I have a feeling you haven't seen the last of him."

The girls watched him wad up his wrappers, unfold himself from his booth and pick up his tray. He nodded slightly as he passed their table, making Jeanette blush all over again.

He was tall. Taller, in fact, than anyone else in the place. She noticed his head brushed the door frame as he walked out of the door. She had to admit he looked good in his worn blue jeans and tan sheepskin coat.

Sandie caught her gaze and laughed. "Ah, so the serious Jeanette is interested in spite of herself."

She chuckled at Jeanette's stumbled protest. Not that it mattered. He would be long gone by the time they were ready to leave. He wasn't.

They found him perched on the hood of their car. "What are you doing here?" Jeanette, demanded then had the decently to blush at her rudeness.

"Waiting for you," he told them.

"Would you please get off the car? We have to be on our way," Jeanette snapped, then wished she hadn't spoken so harshly. He could be dangerous, but she needn't be rude. Still, they knew nothing about this man. Even Sandie hesitated.

Lifting his hands in mock surrender, he said. "Look, I'm not a mass murderer."

Startled, the girls glanced at each other wondering if
he had overheard their earlier conversation. Sandie
asked, "Why are you still here?"

He pointed toward the battered blue pickup next to
their car. The hood was raised. Jeanette kicked herself
for not seeing it immediately. "My pickup won't start. I
wondered if you had jumper cables."

"I think so," Sandie said, heading toward the trunk.
From deep in its interior, she added, "My father won't
let me leave the premises unless I'm fully prepared."

"Including an ancient bike in case the car stalls." He
nodded toward the battered blue three-speed tied onto
the roof."

Jeanette ground out. "That's mine, I'll have you
know. It isn't in any worse shape than that heap of
yours. At least it works and will get me where I need to
go."

Her quick defense brought a boyish grin to the young
man's face--a handsome face, Jeanette decided,
immediately chiding herself for such thoughts.

She gulped when he caught her assessing gaze. "Do I
pass," he whispered softly, chuckling when her face
burned.

Straightening, he put a large hand across his middle
and bowed low. "John Amory at your service. Resident
of McFadden known for its lovely college and
manufacturing."

"That's where we're headed," Sandie said, giving
Jeanette a sidelong wink. "Jeanette is going to college at
ProMark."

"A college freshman? You don't look fresh out of high school."

"I'm not," Jeanette responded, silently pleading with her friend to keep quiet. She should have known her gregarious friend couldn't keep still.

"No," Sandie supplied with obvious pride in her friend. "She went to a community college. She took two years of classes in a year and a half and still managed a 4.0 average."

"Good for you."

Sandie went on, "She was even initiated into the Phi Theta Kappa national honorary."

"What's Phi Theta Kappa?"

"Please, Sandie. Find those cables so we can help him and go." The amused glance he threw her way made her clench her teeth in frustration. Her response to him embarrassed her. Half the time she flushed like some silly school girl with her first crush, and the other half she flushed from sheer fury at his audacity.

In some ways, his nonchalance reminded her sharply of Cynthia. The last thing she needed was to encourage someone like that, but Sandie was on a roll. She rolled her eyes as her friend pulled out the cables as she continued.

"Phi Theta Kappa is the official scholastic honorary for America's two year colleges. You only get in by invitation."

Jeanette cheeks flushed, and she groaned at her friend's chatter. "Listen, John, if that really is your name." His grin widened at this. "If you need help, fine. We'll help you get on your way."

His grin faded under her prim stare. "As you wish, my lady prim." With a brusque nod, he took the cables Sandie dug out of the trunk and attached them to the two vehicles. With Sandie's assistance, he soon had his motor roaring into life. "Thanks, Ladies." His breath whitened in the cold air.

He surveyed Jeanette who stood away from the two cars. "I really won't hurt you, but then you can't know that can you." Jeanette wilted under his gaze. Did she see a hint of reproof in those deep gray eyes?

"John, I...." When a grin stretched his lips, Jeanette bit her lip in frustration.

Smiling his thanks at Sandie, John coiled the cables and replaced them in the trunk for her. "Thank you, ladies." His nod took in Jeanette. "Maybe I'll have to look you up."

Jumping into the cab of his vehicle, he waved as he backed out and headed toward the highway.

Returning his wave, Sandie climbed into the car, followed by Jeanette on the other side. "Sandie, that was foolish. Encouraging him when we don't know anything about him. You know my dad warned us about that."

Sandie grimaced. "My dad, too, and Jeff. Actually, Jeff wanted to come along, but he had to work. I don't think he'll rest easy until I'm home again."

Jeanette laughed. "Nothing did happen. But I was sure praying under my breath. Anyway, it probably doesn't matter, since I doubt I'll ever see him again."

She wondered why the thought did not make her happier.

CHAPTER THREE:

In a more serious frame of mind, the young women turned onto highway 135 south to McFadden. With their separation eminent, there seemed little to talk about. They spent their High School years together, these two, and Jeanette sensed Sandie understood this was not a time for lighthearted banter.

"Jeanette, I'm sorry about that John fellow. I know I handled the situation badly. Me and my big mouth. It never fails to get me into trouble. Only this time, I may have landed you in trouble. What if he really does look you up?"

"I'll deal with that if he does. I'm sure Uncle Silas would help me get rid of him, if needed." With that, she fell silent as she stared out over the plains. Oil wells dotted the landscape intermingling with the beef cattle, grazing in pastures that stretched out for miles without barbed or electric fencing.

A thin crust of snow stretched into the distance, blending with the thick overhanging clouds promising more snow. Jeanette felt the chill even through her new charcoal wool coat.

Sandie noted her shiver. "Sorry about the heater. You know how temperamental it is. Decided to go on the fritz again." She thumped the dashboard that gave an discouraging clunk. Finally, the motor hummed into operation.

"Ah, the magic touch." Sandie tossed her head in mock arrogance.

"God's mercy," Jeanette grunted, hugging her arms to her chest. "He didn't want us to freeze to death."

Their laughter eased the tension, and they talked then as memories surfaced. "What do you hear from Cynthia?" Sandie asked. "I heard she was back for the holidays."

Jeanette hesitated. "Yes, she was back. She got a part in a commercial."

"Wow! I'll have to look for her." A car speeding by took her attention, and by the time it passed, Jeanette pointed to a sign for McFadden.

"Turn off one mile."

The land seemed flatter here. Over the irregular skyline rose a silver water tower proclaiming MCFADDEN in large black letters. To the left they passed the Marsden Refinery with its host of stacks billowing what looked like white clouds against the already lowering sky. Opposite, a huge blinking sign heralded: SORNBORG PLASTICS, largest plastics factory in the state.

"So, what's the address?" Sandie asked, slowing at the first light. As it changed she drove on slowly as she waited for Jeanette's direction.

Picking up her comfortable handbag, Jeanette took out her wallet and pulled out the paper on which she had carefully written her uncle's address. "Here it is. 1531 Maple Drive."

She stared out the window as they passed street after street. Shielding her eyes from the sunlight glaring harshly off banks of snow lining the edges of the street, she read off the street signs as they passed. "There, there it is... Maple street. Turn here, and you'll intersect with Maple Drive."

Checking her mirrors, Sandie carefully made the turn. Another turn and Jeanette stared at the numbers on the houses. It had been forever since she'd visited her aunt and uncle.

"You've been here before, right?"

"Not since I was eight or nine. Usually, Aunt Evelyn and Uncle Silas came out to see us, because Dad was always busy on the farm. Since Dad's accident, Silas comes to help out when he can get away for a couple of days here and there. Wait!" She pointed. "That's it. I'm sure of it."

After pulling into the drive, the two girls got out and stretched. Even before they reached the door, it flew open, and her aunt waved them inside. "Come in. Come in. It's getting cold out here."

Not waiting for Jeanette to shed her coat, Aunt Evelyn wrapped her in a loving embrace. "Jeanette, I'm so glad you're here." Jeanette returned her warm hug before introducing her friend.

"This is my best friend Sandie Marcuson."

"Sandie, my Aunt Evelyn."

Sandie looked startled as she found herself enveloped in the arms of the tall, thin woman. Aunt Evelyn's gray hair softened the lines of her angular face, as did the genuinely welcoming smile. "Welcome, Sandie." Turning her head, Evelyn called, "Silas. Silas, Jeanette's here."

"Auntie, I thought Uncle Silas would still be at the store."

Evelyn laughed. "One of the benefits of being the owner is the ability to take off now and again. Don't you worry. He has good help at the store." Taking their arms, she escorted them into the small, but elegant living room.

Thick carpet cushioned their feet, and large (and Jeanette guessed--valuable) paintings caressed the eyes. While her aunt certainly fit the muted baize decor with its soft, white couch and chair, Uncle Silas seemed out of place as he skirted a Queen Anne table almost knocking over a lamp Jeanette was sure cost a great deal of money.

Deftly, Silas righted the lamp, grinned at his wife who only sighed. Yet her eyes were indulgent and loving. "I was afraid you wouldn't make it before the snow hit." He gave Jeanette a hug that squeezed the breath from her. "Who's your friend," he queried, releasing her.

"Sandie Marcuson. My best friend since high school."

"Marcuson. Your father, is that Harvey Marcuson?"
Sandie nodded. "Yes, it is."

"He owns several stores in northwest Kansas. Right."

"Why, yes he does, Mr. Roberts." Sandie looked surprised. "Do you know of him?"

"Know of him? You bet I know him. In fact, I've done business with him. He's a good, honest Christian man. And I'm glad to meet his daughter. Sandie, wasn't it?" He pumped her hand. "Now, about your things."

"Oh, we can bring them in, Uncle Silas."

"No, I'll take care of that."

Sandie glanced toward Jeanette and shrugged as Silas swung out the door to bring in Jeanette's luggage and Sandie's overnight bag. "Auntie, you don't mind Sandie staying overnight, do you?"

Her aunt's eyebrows raised. "Of course not. I'm just glad you didn't have to come alone. I was afraid you'd bring that old farm truck your father got working."

She led the way down the short hall out of which opened two bedrooms and a bath. You'll sleep here, dear, for now. Later, if you prefer, you can take one of the larger bedrooms downstairs. We don't use them much these days. With the kids gone, we hardly even go down there anymore, except when they come home."

"I'm sure this will be fine." Jeanette surveyed the wood-paneled room. A thick, rich blue comforter covered the double bed with its shelf headboard set against the far corner. The shelves were a perfect place for her books. Sliding doors near the foot of the bed opened to reveal a closet, and the other corner held a desk with a high intensity lamp.

"It looks like this was set up just for me." Turning, she caught the guilty smile on the face of her uncle who stood in the doorway his arms loaded down with her luggage.

"You did, didn't you?" Tears stung her eyes. "Thank you." Overwhelmed at their generosity, she hugged her aunt and uncle all over again.

Silas struggled under her embrace. "Better let me set these down before I drop them on your toes," he growled.

Giggling, Jeanette kissed his cheek. "All right. I'll get out of the way." She winked at her aunt as she stepped back, knowing her uncle's bluntness hid a soft heart.

Silas set the baggage on the bed. "Get on with you, Jeanette," he said, his tone gruff.

Aunt Evelyn added, "We wanted you to feel at home."

"Now that you are here safe and sound," Silas said, clearing his throat, "I might as well go on back to the store."

Her aunt walked with him back into the living room. In the distance, Jeanette heard her say, "Oh, Silas, I'd like you to bring home some ice cream."

Jeanette smiled when he grunted, "Ice cream, in this weather? Oh, all right." Pause. "It's starting to snow."

"You take care, Silas. Remember, dinner at six."

"I will dear."

Sandie shook her head. "Your uncle rather scares me."

"Don't let him." Jeanette laughed. "He's blunt and gruff, but he's a teddy bear really. I can't believe as often as they've been out to visit us, you've never met. Strange isn't it."

Sandie waved her arms. "Strange things are beginning to happen," she moaned, then jumped as the wind echoed her moan.

Jeanette collapsed onto the bed giggling. "You should have seen the look on your face right now. Serves you right for being spooky."

Grabbing a pillow, Sandie threw it at her friend.

The snow continued throughout the evening, the wind rising to swirl it against the windows. The girls could hear the moan of the wind as they lay in bed later that night. "I hope it will settle before morning," Sandie said in a hushed tone. "I have to get home. Jeff and I have plans."

"Then let's pray about it," Jeanette said, stifling a yawn.

They awoke to a silent wonderland of fantasy forms shaped by the wind. Coming out of their bedroom, they heard the scrape of a shovel on the drive. Hearing them, Evelyn called from the kitchen. "Ready for breakfast?"

They followed her voice through the open living room, through the dining room to the kitchen area, separated from the dining area by a long breakfast bar. They found Evelyn standing over a sizzling skillet filled with bacon.

"Aunt Evelyn, you needn't," Jeanette protested. "We should be fixing breakfast for you and Uncle Silas. Since it's Saturday, I didn't think anyone would be up this early." She glanced at the clock on the microwave cart by the refrigerator It read nine.

Her aunt smiled. "Silas seldom takes time off on Saturday. He has to make certain everything is running smoothly."

Sandie added, "I thought he had competent help."

"Oh, he does, dear, but he likes to feel needed." Aunt Evelyn expertly turned the bacon. "And there is a great deal to do."

Hearing the roar of the grader, the girls went to the window. Jeanette eyed the thick snow. "Maybe I should go out and help scoop."

"Me too," Sandie said, but was interrupted as Silas heaved his bulk into the door and shook off the snow onto the thick pile.

"No need. All finished," he told them.

"Do you think I'll be able to get home today?" Sandie asked as worry lit her face.

Shrugging out of his heavy coat, Silas hung it on the coat rack by the door. "Oh, I think so. The main roads are already pretty well open. There's a good deal of snow, but little ice. I think you can leave safely in a couple more hours."

Brring, Brring rang the phone. Evelyn answered it. "Yes, yes she is."

"Sandie, it's for you."

Sandie groaned as she took the cordless. "I bet he tried my cell first, but I left it in the bedroom."

"Her young man, I think. Now for the rest of you, breakfast time."

Sandie returned to the kitchen as Jeanette dug into her scrambled eggs and bacon. "Well?"

Taking another plateful, Sandie sat beside Jeanette at the breakfast bar. "Jeff is going to meet me in Hays. I told him I'd be on my way by ten."

She was. Jeanette saw her off with distinct trepidation. Yes, she was concerned about her friend traveling in snow, but it was more than that. Sandie was a part of her life, and with her departure, Jeanette felt her past slipping away. She began to realize how sheltered she'd been. Her family seldom traveled, and home had been security for her. The parting with Sandie portended a new life for her.

Exhilaration vied with fear for supremacy, homesickness with the thirst for change, for adventure for ...the possibilities were endless, and Jeanette was not sure how to handle all the new emotions surfacing. She valued the steadying influence of her aunt and uncle.

The rest of Saturday passed quietly. By afternoon, the sun scuttled the clouds and sparkled on the snow. The road turned into dirty mush as vehicles roared up and down. Rivulets of water streamed down the ditches. By sundown, the temperature dropped sharply turning slush into sheets of ice.

Jeanette spent a quiet evening with her aunt and uncle. Getting acclimated to the kitchen, Jeanette popped popcorn for them all, before they sat down before the television to watch the movie Silas purchased for them. By nine o'clock Jeanette was in her room, readying herself for bed.

After putting her things away, she made a quick call to her folks. From the desk, she picked up her Bible. Feeling lonely despite the welcome of her aunt and uncle, Jeanette flipped it open, seeking comfort as well as direction. Psalms 27 caught her eye and she read, "The Lord is my light and my salvation; whom shall I fear? The Lord is the strength of my life; of whom shall I be afraid."

Her life was in the Lord's hands. Wherever she was, He would be her strength. Bowing her head, she prayed for her parents, her aunt and uncle, Sandie, her new life and even for her sister.

The next morning, dressed in a soft rose dress with a high neck and full sleeves she had made for herself just before Christmas, Jeanette entered the kitchen as her uncle and aunt were finishing their own breakfast.

"I'm sorry I'm late. I overslept."

Her aunt got up to get her breakfast, but Jeanette forestalled her. "That's all right, Auntie, I don't want to make you late for church."

Taking a still warm biscuit from the plate on the table, she added butter and her aunt's homemade jam, before popping it into her mouth. By the time she finished, her aunt handed her a glass of milk to wash it down. "There. Let me brush my teeth, and I'm ready to go."

Behind her uncle who held the arm of her aunt, Jeanette tentatively entered the unpretentious church building with its tall, narrow steeple. She smiled hesitantly as they introduced her right and left to their acquaintances including Rev. & Mrs. Connors and their twins Josh and Jessica. Proudly, and much to her chagrin, her uncle proclaimed her academic prowess.

Grinning, Joshua took her hand. "Delighted to meet you, Jeanette Roberts. Jess and I are a year behind you, but we'll be glad to show you the ropes, so to speak, at the college." He ran his words and sentences together and spoke so fast, she had trouble following his train of thought.

Jessica broke in. "We're real glad to meet you Jeanette. You will come to youth group Wednesday night. We have a terrific college group. We call ourselves Paul's Marks. You know, mark of a Christian, ProMark."

The twins' constant stream of chatter left her head reeling. Jeanette was relieved when the organist began to play and she was able to sit down with her aunt and uncle.

The lean song leader opened the hymnal. "Let us stand and sing number 103, Blessed Be the Name.

Jeanette automatically looked up expecting an overhead. There was none. She fumbled for a hymnal and flipped open the pages.

As she stood, she sensed someone slip in beside her. Automatically, she offered to share her hymnal only to hear a soft familiar chuckle. Glancing up, the song died in her throat as she met the amused gaze of John Amory.

CHAPTER FOUR:

Jeanette, attired in navy slacks and the sweater given
to her at Christmas, hurried from the three-story red
brick administration building to her class in American
History across campus.

"Whoa!" The dark haired girl exclaimed as Jeanette
rounded a corner, her eyes on the schedule in her hand.

Blushing, Jeanette stepped back. "Oh, I am sorry.
Guess I wasn't paying much attention to where I was
going." Glancing down at her schedule, she grimaced.
"Not that this helps much."

Picking up the book she dropped when Jeanette
bumped into her, the short, but well-formed young
woman surveyed her up and down. "Let's see. Slender,
blue-eyed and lost. My guess...you're new here, right?"

"Good guess." Jeanette giggled, grimaced. "It shows,
doesn't it?"

"Surely you're not a freshman? You don't look it."

"No, I'm a junior. I attended a community college in
my hometown, but it wasn't anything like this," she
commented. "The community college was certainly
smaller, and it took hardly any time at all before I knew
my way around."

The other girl laughed. "I know what you mean, but
this isn't bad at all. After one year of community

college, I tried Kansas State. If you think this is big." She rolled her eyes. "After one semester there, I transferred here. That was last year.

"By the way, my name is Darilyn Summers. From Blue Rapids. My dad has a dairy there."

"I'm Jeanette Roberts. My dad has a farm near Colby. We raise Herefords, corn, some milo and wheat mostly."

"I think I'm going to like you, Jeanette Roberts." Darilyn hooked her arm through Jeanette's. "Come on, I'll show you around." And she did.

Making her way purposefully across campus, Jeanette breathed a prayer of thanks for Darilyn. Acting as guide, she gave Jeanette such a thorough tour that Jeanette soon felt she could find her way blindfolded. Well, almost.

After being accosted by the twins, both of whom seldom stopped talking long enough to take a breath and constantly interrupted each other with no hint of rancor, Jeanette continued on with a certain relief. Both Jess and Josh were likable enough, but exhausting.

Seeing them, reminded her of her embarrassment Sunday when she discovered John at her side. She flushed at his whisper. "Hope you're not disappointed to find I'm not a mass murderer after all." His deep chuckle curled her toes. "Why, most of these fine folk consider me down right respectable."

He really must have overheard them talking! Embarrassment vied with fury within her. Fury won. The nerve of him to tease her about being cautious. She felt like snatching back the hymnal, but decided that would only amuse him further. Why did she have to sit with him for the duration of the service?

His nearness made it difficult for her to concentrate on the sermon. Covertly, she watched him, unable to understand the confusion of her emotions as his arm brushed hers. She was impressed when he found the place in his large study Bible with the ease of long practice. She had her own Bible, but wished for a smart phone with a Bible app. How convenient that would be.

Catching her glance, John smiled. He had a nice smile, if only his eyes didn't dance with such devilment. Magnanimously Jeanette decided to forgive him, until after the service when he introduced her to his mother, a slip of woman whose pale face and trembling hands, proclaimed her ill health.

"Mother, may I introduce you to Miss Jeanette Roberts." His lips turned up wickedly. "She and her friend helped get the old rig going at a truck stop in Salina." He paused dramatically. "They helped out even though she suspected me of being some kind of criminal."

The woman's smile wavered a moment as Jeanette protested, wishing she could hide her tell-tale cheeks. To her further embarrassment, her aunt and uncle overheard and turned toward them "What's this, John. A murderer--of a joke maybe," her Uncle chided.

Gratefully, Aunt Evelyn stood up for her. "Jeanette was right to be careful of you. There are far too many reports of young women being taken in by some fiendish

charmer, then raped or murdered." Evelyn tapped John
on the arm. "You are a charmer, John Amory."

John's eyes actually twinkled as they glanced toward
Jeanette. "I doubt your niece would agree. I guess we'll
have to work on that."

Uncle Silas nodded. "Well, now that you two have
been introduced properly, you'll probably be seeing
quite a lot of each other."

Not if she could help it! Jeanette stared up at her
uncle. If he planned on matchmaking, she had
something to say about that! "I don't think...."

She never did get to finish the sentence. Aunt Evelyn
invited the Amorys for dinner and there was nothing she
could do about it. Her innate manners exerted
themselves. She sensed John wanted to take her arm, but
instead he took his mother's elbow. Jeanette was rather
touched at the way he carefully helped his mother from
the church into an old green and gold car.

Anger strove with another emotion she could not
name, admiration maybe? But why was she angry;
maybe because of his amusement at her expense or from
another emotion she refused to name? Truthfully, she
wondered if her anger was directed more at John--or
herself.

Later that evening, she sat before the fireplace
watching its flickering light play over the faces of her
aunt and uncle and feeling its warmth. Aunt Evelyn's
knitting needles clicked from the speed at which she
worked.

"What are you making, Aunt Evelyn? I like the colors. They look like baby slippers."

"They are." Momentarily, Aunt Evelyn halted her work and held up the little booties. "I make these for the children at the hospital," she said. "I like knitting booties for the babies and slippers for the older children. I remember how cold and lonely a hospital can seem sometimes." Jeanette caught her Uncle's eye. She hadn't meant to remind her aunt of the child they lost many years earlier.

Jeanette asked, not only to change the subject, but also because she was curious about John and his mother. "What's wrong with Mrs. Amory?"

Uncle Silas explained, "Mrs. Amory has been a widow for many years, but her husband left before that. Until the last few years, she held a good job as a secretary out at the Marsden refinery."

"Ill health forced her to quit," her aunt said. "Not that they had much before that."

"John took right over," Silas added. There was no doubt of his admiration for the young man. "He works hard and is as honest as you find them. Even without a degree, he'll go places." He took in his niece as though seeing her for the first time as a young woman.

"I don't think I'd be out of line to tell you, I think he likes what he sees in you, Jeanette." He chuckled and Jeanette knew, even without a word, he was reminded of her suspicions of John.

Her blush drew her aunt's censure. "Now Silas, leave the girl alone. She did what was right."

"Of course she did," he agreed, but his eyes still twinkled.

She was not sure how she felt about the young man. As she walked toward class, she recalled John's deep chuckle in her mind and felt a shiver slide down her back. She hated the way she responded to him. For all her uncle assured her of John's proven record of responsibility, she couldn't help but compare him to Cynthia. And yet....

Ahead, the long low building that housed the history and economics departments beckoned. Around her, laughter and quiet voices mingled with the crunch of snow underfoot as other students hurried to their classes. Shifting her book bag to her other shoulder, she stamped her high topped boots over the hard ridge of snow toward the door. The sun shown down on the snow so brightly it dazzled the eyes, yet created little warmth. Jeanette was grateful for the warmth of her gloves, a gift from Sandie for Christmas.

Just inside the door, she stopped to let her eyes adjust to the seemingly dim interior. "Jeanette." Darilyn waved to her. "This way. Hurry, we're almost late."

Jeanette hurried into the building and down the hall with Darilyn.

Taking their seats, Darilyn rolled her eyes at the professor who strode through the door. "Oh no! Miss Tornbloom." Darilyn groaned, but softly, for Jeanette's benefit. She made it sound like a disease.

The stout, solidly-build woman strode, not walked. Barked, not talked, and reminded Jeanette of an upended traveling trunk. The woman's rough manner was something she had not expected at a Christian college, and she could not still her soft gasp fast enough.

When the student in the desk in front of her turned around, she found herself lost in the deepest, most beautiful blue eyes she had ever seen. For a moment she forgot where she was until the smile of sympathy on the young man's face made her realize Miss Tornbloom had caught her out.

"Miss... What is your name please?" she barked, punctuating her question with her pointer.

"Miss Jeanette Roberts." Jeanette's smile faded under the woman's glare.

Consulting a computer printout in her hand, the large woman said. "Ah, yes, a transfer student I see. Well, Miss Roberts. This is not a social club, but history, college history. We do not gawk in class." She turned to the lesson then, but for Jeanette it was far too late.

Tears sprang to her eyes, but she blinked them back. Her cheeks bloomed like a summer rose. At her left, she sensed Darilyn's sympathy, but all she could think of was that she had disgraced herself in front of the student in front of her, the one with gorgeous blue eyes and the devastating smile.

Though she made sure to follow the lesson, her eyes kept straying to the young man sitting in front of her. His smile had been kind, not mocking like John's. His blond hair rippled down to his neck in delightful waves.

She wondered if they were natural and blushed at the urge to run her fingers through his hair.

His wide shoulders fitted nicely in the well-tailored blazer he wore over an open necked shirt. Jeanette thought, Monogrammed, no doubt.

After class, she gathered up her books and stuffed them into her bag. Before she picked up her coat from where she had slung it on the back of the chair, the young man with the deep blue eyes held it out for her.

"Thank you," Jeanette managed, wondering why her knees seemed suddenly weak. She caught Darilyn's dazed stare.

"I'm Brad Marsden," the young man said. "And you're Jeanette Roberts. Jeanette. Jeanette." He rolled the name around on his tongue. "I like it. Well, Miss Jeanette Roberts. How about sharing lunch with me?"

Jeanette glanced at Darilyn uncertainly. "I promised Darilyn."

Brad surveyed the other girl. "Yes, well, you wouldn't mind if I appropriated your friend for lunch do you?" It really wasn't a question, and for a moment, Jeanette resented his arrogant manner, until she stared into the smiling face and lost her train of thought.

"Ah, no. I guess...not." Darilyn managed to stutter as Brad took Jeanette's arm and led her from the room.

Jeanette found herself the center of attention in the cafeteria where she sat at a small corner table with Brad. She didn't miss the envious looks thrown their way, especially from several young women.

Jeanette ate her fries, her forehead creased in thought. "Marsden. Marsden as of Marsden Refinery?"

"The same. My father's company, and, one day-- mine." Brad made it not a boast, but a simple statement of truth.

"I see." Jeanette wasn't sure how to handle the situation. She felt out of place in her homemade clothes with the son of one of the wealthiest men in town.

Brad's soft smile broke through her reserve. "So tell me about yourself, Jeanette Roberts. Where are you from?"

"My parents have a farm near Colby. As for me..." Before she knew it, Jeanette found herself explaining about her father's accident.

"That must have been difficult for you." Brad squeezed her hand lightly. His sympathy warmed something within her. "I admire your courage in making something of yourself despite all your setbacks."

For all Brad's seeming sympathy, Jeanette felt a certain condescension on his part that bothered her. Then again, she told herself, she was probably being oversensitive.

"May I ask why you decided to stay and attend college in McFadden." She felt the flush on her cheeks. She might as well have said, "Since you're so filthy rich, why aren't you attending Harvard or Yale."

He picked up her hand and squeezed it gently as though he understood and was not offended. "I need to learn the business from the ground up. I can't do that from a distance. I'll get my degree in business right here. I'm just thankful ProMark offers the degree. My grandfather saw to that."

"Your grandfather?"

"Yes, grand old man. He's gone now, but I've always admired his drive to make something of himself, like my great grandfather. He helped found this town, this college too. Did you know that ProMark will be 100 years old this year?"

Shaking her head, Jeanette told him. "I had no idea. You must be very proud of your family and what they've done for the town."

"Of course. I and someday my wife," he looked at her in a way that made her breath stop, "will continue the Marsden family line and traditions."

Not knowing how to respond, Jeanette was thankful when Brad steered the conversation to lighter subjects. "So, what do you do for fun."

"I haven't had much time to do anything more than find my way around campus," she said with a laugh. "Fun is going to be school and church and work and study."

"All work and no play, makes Jack...or Jeanette a very dull person." Brad's eyes lit up with laughter. "And we certainly can't permit that to happen. Tell you what, Jeanette Roberts." He tapped a finger on her nose. "I have the perfect solution."

"I'm afraid to ask, but what do you have in mind?"

"Let me tell you...."

By the time they finished their lunch, Jeanette found she had accepted a date for a movie Friday night with

Brad Marsden, a man she had just met and knew next to nothing about. What's more, she didn't care.

CHAPTER FIVE:

Brad picked her up promptly at five in a low-slung, black sports car. Aunt Evelyn seemed pleased Brad asked her out. "Nice young man," she said with a smile, throwing a look toward Silas Jeanette could not interpret. "I dare say, you'll be the envy of every other girl on campus--and then some."

"Money isn't the measure of a man," Silas grunted. "What about the Sornborg girl? I heard the two were all but engaged. You know the families always assumed they'd get together."

"Harrumph," Evelyn said. "Maybe he's wised up. He can't be all that bad if he saw Jeanette's worth."

Jeanette felt her cheeks flush at this conversation. Seeking to derail it, she asked. "Who is this Sornborg girl, you're talking about?"

Her uncle opened his mouth, then closed it again at the frown on his wife's face. "Antonia, Tony, Sornborg is the daughter...."

Suddenly recalling the sign as she came into town, Jeanette added, "Sornborg Plastics, right?"

Silas looked relieved. "That's right."

"Does she go to ProMark, too?"

Her aunt shook her head. "Oh, no. A hometown college is much too provincial for Miss Sornborg. She

wanted to go to some hoity-toity school out east, but her
father said she had to support her own state. She's a
sophomore or junior at Kansas State University at
Manhattan."

"Brad is older then. He said he's a senior, but he's
going on for his masters in business."

Aunt Evelyn commented, "He also took a year off
after high school to travel."

Jeanette's eyes widened. "I didn't know that. He did
say his father would like for him to go to the University
for a Doctorate, but Brad would rather help run the
refinery. He says the rest of his education can come
later."

Her uncle tilted his head. "Not bad thinking on his
part." He seemed reluctant to admit it.

"Is there some reason you don't like Brad, Uncle
Silas?" Jeanette asked. "Is there any reason I shouldn't
go out with him?"

"You're caught now, Silas," her aunt chortled,
before turning to her niece. "Jeanette, it isn't that your
uncle doesn't like the Marsden boy, it's just that he'd
rather play matchmaker between you and a certain
young man we had over for dinner last Sunday. Isn't that
right, dear?"

Glaring at his wife in mock anger, Silas faced
Jeanette, a sheepish grin on his face. "John's a nice
young man. You could do worse."

Jeanette laughed and gave him a hug. "Oh, Uncle
Silas, you're as bad as my parents. However," she told

him sternly, "I'd prefer to find my own husband, if you don't mind."

He grinned like a mischievous boy, a look not unlike the look she'd seen in John's eyes. "We'll see. We'll see." He shifted gears. "Now that you've gotten into the school routine, you ready to get started at the store?"

Evelyn shook her head in warning. "Silas..."

"You lead the way, and I'll follow," Jeanette said. "I'm anxious to get started paying my way, Uncle Silas."

"You know that's not why I'm giving you a job. You are not to pay us back for anything. We want you as part of our family. But I also know you have other expenses--personal and school. I'm glad I can offer you a job."

Her job was the furthermost thing from her mind as she slipped onto the leather seat of Brad's car. She hoped her textured jade silk chemise dress was appropriate attire for the evening. Adjusting her legs to the low seat, she smoothed the silky material over her knees. Despite her confidence in her ability as a seamstress, she wondered if anything handmade would pass the inspection of her date, breathtakingly handsome in a navy suit and silk shirt. From her own sense of style and knowledge of fashion, Jeanette recognized the finest of tailoring and material.

At his frankly admiring gaze, her confidence rose, even as her breath stopped. "You are a vision." He studied her again. "From what you told me of your background, I would not have expected you to dress with such style. Have you a fairy godmother somewhere?"

Relaxing, Jeanette laughed. "Not at all." Fingering the dress, she wondered if she should hold back the truth, then blurted. "Actually, I designed and made it myself."

He glanced at her in surprise. Did she mistake the sudden tightening of his hands on the wheel? "Yourself? I would not have guessed. Hmm. You're very talented."

Less sure, Jeanette told him. "I'm getting a degree in Family and Consumer Science with a minor in art. I hope to teach, but I also want to design my own clothing."

Brad nodded and for several moments, neither spoke. As though making a decision, the frown on his face lifted. "At least you're getting on with your education. That's important."

"It is if you want to teach." She melted under his devastating smile.

"Teach. Yes, well, things do change."

When they passed the city limits, she asked, "Where are we going?"

She tensed as the car growled into life like a living being when Brad pressed down on the gas. With some trepidation, Jeanette watched the speedometer climb. Brad grinned at her obvious concern.

"Don't worry; I'm careful to stay within the legal speed limit. Since you asked, we're going to this little place I know of in Hutchinson."

The rest of the trip, Jeanette sat back and listened as Brad regaled her with stories about his family and all the benefits they bestowed on the town. No doubt, he felt strongly about his family's position. At times, Jeanette felt rather insignificant beside him and was glad when they turned into the restaurant parking lot.

The little place turned out to be an elegant Victorian-style restaurant that made Jeanette feel she had no business entering its doors. From all the attention they showed Brad, it was obvious not only that they knew him, but also that he ate here often. The glances the other patrons threw her way were bright with unspoken curiosity.

With gentlemanly concern, Brad seated her, but neglected to consult her about her preferences before ordering.

The stiff-backed waiter wearing an equaling stiff looking tuxedo stood, pad in hand, at their table. "Drinks?"

"Jeanette?" Brad asked, "Do you care for wine with your meal?"

She stared at him in mute shock. Closing the huge engraved menu, Brad shook his head. "I guess not, Wayne. Tea will be fine." He paused. "For both of us."

He went on to order what seemed like a fantastic amount of food. When the waiter left them, he surveyed Jeanette. "I'm sorry if I shocked you, Jeanette. I did not mean to, but I didn't know how you felt about such things. Most people, even Christians, indulge now and again these days."

"I don't," she whispered and wondered why it hurt so much to admit something she had been adamant about all her life.

Brad patted her hand. "Not at all?"

"Not at all." She held her breath.

"Of course not. I didn't think. Forgive me." Jeanette relaxed then, and the dinner progressed with Brad telling her about his work, his schooling and his ambitions.

She appreciated his serious manner, very unlike John's. With disgust she put John from her mind. There was no comparison between the serious, sensitive Brad and the brash, teasing John.

Brad was waiting indulgently for her to finish her Bavarian Cream pie when a willowy blond sauntered over to them. Jeanette's eyes widened when the curvaceous blond leaned over and kissed Brad on the lips. "Brad, dear. I didn't expect to find you here. Why didn't you call?" She completely ignored Jeanette's presence.

"I had no idea you were home for the weekend, Tony."

Jeanette's heart sunk. So this was the girl everyone expected Brad to marry. Jeanette felt herself withdraw. She certainly was no competition for the women in her shimmering low-cut gown.

Her face flushed as Brad turned attention toward her. "Tony, I'd like you to meet, Jeanette Roberts. She's a junior at ProMark; just transferred in."

"How k-i-n-d of you to show her around Brad." Jeanette shriveled under her contemptuous gaze that took in every detail of her person and clothing. Jeanette flushed, sure the woman knew the exact origin of her dress.

Brad rescued her with a curt, "Cut it out, Tony. Be a good girl and be on your way. Surely you're not here alone."

Jeanette straightened. If Tony, too, was dating someone else, the two couldn't be serious about each other.

"You will call tomorrow?"

"If I have time," Brad told her firmly. His eyes softened at Jeanette's distress. "Come on. No reason to let anyone else spoil our evening." His smile erased Jeanette's embarrassment. "Don't let Tony intimidate you, Jeanette. You're every bit as lovely as she is and much more natural." The way he said it, Jeanette wondered if he meant that for a compliment, but decided he must have meant it that way. Why else would he say anything at all?

By the time they arrived home after the movie, Jeanette had all but forgotten Tony. If there had been something between the two of them, it was over or Brad could surely not looked at her the way he did on the ride home. More than once, he reached out to touch her cheek and squeeze her hand. "Will you attend church with me Sunday?"

"I don't think so, Brad. My aunt and uncle expect me to attend with them, and I am staying with them."

"I understand. How about Sunday night, can I have you then?"

"I suppose that would be all right." Jeanette's heart thumped. Brad liked her!

At the door, ever so gently, he pressed his lips to hers. Her mother and father brought her up with Christian principles, and she knew even kisses were not to be given lightly, but when he brought her home it seemed so right somehow. It was only a kiss after all. If true, why did she float into the house and go to sleep with the story of Cinderella on her mind?

Saturday she insisted on cleaning the house for Aunt Evelyn who protested, then acquiesced, admitting she was rather tired. After lunch, Uncle Silas took her down to the store.

"The largest grocery store in the area," he boasted, as he parked the car. "I started with a small little store right on this location. Now I not only have this one, but three others: one in Hutch, one in McPherson and one in Salina. That's where my manager is today. He'll be back Monday to settle you in. While he's gone, I have to see everything runs smoothly, you know." He winked at his niece.

As her uncle showed her around, Jeanette was impressed not only with the size of the store, but also with the care and concern her uncle had shown for each detail. "Very accessible."

"I want to make my stores friendly for my elderly customers and others that have difficulties with stairs or narrow aisles."

He also proudly introduced her to some of the staff. "You know Josh, here."

Josh waved as he carried out a bag of groceries for an elderly woman. "Does Jessica also work here."

"No. Believe it or not, Jessica flatly refused to work in the same store with her brother. Something about a separate identity. Frankly," he lowered his voice, "I was delighted. When the two of them are together..."

Jeanette giggled. "I understand. I like them, too, but it's exhausting listening to them."

"That's about the size of it." He nodded. "You'll be working here at the counter. Hope you're good at figures."

"We...ll. I certainly can't claim math as my best subject."

"Oh you'll do fine." He patted her hand.

She hoped he was right.

Later that night, she opened her books and sighed. After one week of school she already had more assignments than she thought possible. Actually, only History concerned her. After her beginning with Miss Tornbloom, who assigned a paper due on Monday, of at least five pages, on the first settlements in America, she knew she had to do her best.

Settling down on her comfortable bed, she opened the books she picked up from the college library Friday after school and began to read. By ten, she had her report entered on the refurbished tablet with a keyboard she'd been able to purchase. She still needed to print the report out. She'd worry about that tomorrow.

How she wished she had the funds for a laptop and a printer. *Lord?*

Rubbing her eyes, Jeanette closed her books and put them away. Taking her nightgown, robe, towel and toiletries, she made her way downstairs to take a long hot bath where she would not inconvenience her aunt and uncle. Two bathrooms in the house was a luxury she could easily get used to.

Lying back, she let her mind wonder. Touching her lips, she smiled, remembering her first real kiss. Unlike other girls her age, she early determined to keep herself for her husband alone. Yet, Brad's kiss seemed so right at the time. For a moment John's face came to mind, but she forced it away. Brad.... Maybe fairy tales did come true.

Back upstairs later, she sat down on her bed. Yawning, she looked at her Bible laying on the desk. Every night since she was a little girl she read her Bible before she slept, but she was so tired. Surely it wouldn't hurt to forget just once. Tomorrow was Sunday, which meant Bible study. Just before she dropped off to sleep, she realized it meant something else, John.

John managed to once more sit beside her in the church service, and, once more, Jeanette found herself forced into sharing a hymnal with him. When it came time to look up the passage of scripture, Jeanette guiltily realized she had forgotten her Bible. With but a hint of a smile, John shared his own. The Bible, though newer than her own, was much annotated and underlined, telling Jeanette John was a serious Bible student.

Serious? Somehow the word didn't seem to apply to John. Her mind wondered to Brad.

After the service, Josh and Jess approached. She had a hard time keeping her face straight when John whispered, "here come the twin mouths."

"Jeanette," Jessica started. "We'd like you to come to our meeting tonight."

"We're having a Paul's Marks meeting tonight," added Josh before Jessica took a breath.

"You will come won't you." Jess added. "I know you're busy and all, but ....

"We missed you Wednesday night," Josh continued. "I thought you said you'd come."

Jeanette held up her hand. "I'm sorry, I totally forgot Wednesday. As for tonight, I'm afraid not. I already made other plans." She thought of her date with Brad, if you called attending an evening service with him, a date.

This Sunday, John walked her to the car. "Where is your mother?"

"Not feeling well today."

Jeanette's concern elicited a slight smile."Nothing serious, I hope."

"She'll be all right," he assured her, but without much conviction. "Sorry you can't make it tonight. How about if I pick you up Wednesday night?"

Not able to think of any excuse, Jeanette agreed, though reluctantly. She sensed John knew exactly why she hesitated, and it galled her. "Good." He grinned. "I'll see you tomorrow."

Jeanette glanced up at him through the door of the car. "Tomorrow? I didn't think you went to college."

He chuckled. "I don't. I mean, I'll see you after school, at the store."

"What!"

This time he laughed out right. "You don't know then."

"Know what? Do you work at the store?" Please, Lord, no.

"I'm your uncle's manager. I am the one he appointed to get you started."

With a grin, he shut the door, leaving Jeanette staring after him in dismay.

CHAPTER SIX:

The next couple of weeks went by in a blur of
school, work and activities. For all her fears about
working with John Amory, she found him an exacting,
but patient boss.

Her cheeks burned, recalling all the mistakes she
made that first week. She still had no idea why it took so
long for her to understand how the register worked. It
was simple enough once she understood. That first
Saturday, her first full day of work, things went from
bad to disaster.

In fact, she had to call John over to help her so often,
Josh teased her. "Sure it isn't the manager, rather than
the job you're after."

She bit her lip in frustration at the friendly jest. From
the looks on the faces of the other women checkers, she
was sure the thought had already crossed their minds.
But when she heard John's chuckle behind her, it almost
proved too much.

Seeing the tears springing to her eyes, John took
charge. "They'll be enough. Jeanette is new here. Can
any of you claim you had less trouble getting this all
down?"

Lowering their eyes, the other checkers turned away.
Josh plopped down on the countertop in front of her.

"Sorry, Jeanette, I was just kidding, not that John here isn't a good catch, if you go for the rugged type. Maybe you'd rather have a younger man." He puffed out his chest. "Your beauty absolutely dazzles me, Jeanette. Have pity on me."

Laughing, Jeanette pushed him off the counter. "Get out of here." Nonetheless, his lightheartedness took the sting from the incident.

John frowned at Josh, "Now look here, Son." He postured. "There'll not be those kinds of goings on in this store." Next, he leaned over the counter, his face close to Jeanette's, his eyes sparkling with mischief. "If the lovely checker would consider having lunch with the manager, now that is entirely different."

Jeanette vied between laughter and fury at his temerity. After a pause she asked, "And if I say no?"

He grinned, "I'll ask again...later."

With a sweet smile, she said, "And if I call it sexual harassment?"

He straightened quickly. Tone cold as ice, he said, "I'm sorry if I offended you, Miss Roberts."

Jeanette would have given anything to wipe the hurt from his eyes. She well knew he meant no harm, but he stalked away even as she tried to stutter an apology.

Josh shook his head. "Did you lay it on or what? Remind me not to tangle with you." He left her feeling uncertain.

Next time she needed help, she dreaded asking for him. In fact, she didn't ask until she jammed up the register and the customer complained. "If I had known

how incompetent you were, I would have used one of
the other checkers." The balding businessman nervously
rubbed his arm. "I am on my lunch hour, and I'm in a
hurry." He glanced toward the next aisle. "Maybe I'll
move down."

"I am truly sorry, Sir." Lifting up the phone with a
trembling hand, she paged John. Trying not to shift from
one foot to the other, Jeanette waited as impatiently as
her disgruntled customer for the manager. Without
closing her eyes, and while keeping a forced smile on
her lips, Jeanette sent up a prayer for help.

If her uncle learned about her incompetence he
would have no other choice, but to fire her. *Thank you,
Lord, Uncle Silas isn't in town today, but at one of his
other stores. At least, he can't fire me today. Can John?
Oh no! Lord, if I get fired, where will I get the money to
finish college?* She had visions of returning home a total
and utter failure.

When John arrived, she couldn't help the sudden
jump in her pulse rate or her gratitude as he quickly took
over. "What's the problem here, Mr. Karlsson?"

The businessman calmed in the face of John's
competence and willingness to assist. With a deft touch
of humor, John quickly unscrambled the mess. Standing
by, Jeanette was amazed at how easily John not only
soothed the customer, but actually had the man laughing
at the situation. Not only that, the man actually
apologized.

"Sorry for giving you a bad time, but next time, Miss," the man said with a grin, "I'll expect you to be right on top of things."

"Thank you, sir," she stuttered. "I'll do my best."

After personally escorting the man to the door, John returned to Jeanette. Taking her arm, he led her into his office at the back of the store. Gulping back tears, Jeanette dragged after him. This was it. She was getting fired.

Raising her head as they entered the small plain room containing a desk, she absently noticed the sparse furnishings, a four drawer file, a worn chair behind the desk and a folding chair against the wall. Behind the desk, a sign said, "No smoking please."

If she was going to be fired, at least she would be dignified about it. Instead, after closing the door, John led her to the folding chair and set her down. "Just sit there a minute. I'll be right back."

He returned with two cans of pop and sandwiches and chips from the deli. Setting them on the desk, he sat down in the desk chair. "Now pull up your chair and eat."

"How could you?" Jeanette bit her lip. "This is horrible."

Baffled, John stared at her as though she'd lost her senses. "Now what did I do wrong?"

Despite her best efforts, Jeanette burst into tears. "How could you act so nice just be...before you f...ire me?"

"Fire you!" John thundered, sounding very much like her uncle. "Whatever gave you the cork-brained idea I was going to fire you?"

"But...but. I'm an awful checker. I can't get anything right. I said dreadful things to you and hurt your feelings when I knew you didn't mean any harm..."

John looked pained. "If I fired everyone who hurt my feelings, I'd be running this place alone, and your uncle would find himself another manager."

"But you brought me back here." She sniffed, "I thought...."

Throwing up his hands, John asked, "Jeanette, have you always been so serious?"

She resented his tone, but only shook her head. "Not always," she said, thinking of her sister's defection.

"There's hope then." There was the beginning of a smile on his tight lips. "I brought you back here," he told her slowly, "because you were falling apart out there. Not good for business, not good at all. You needed a break." He smiled more broadly.

"Besides, now, while you collect yourself, we're sharing the lunch I offered. Unless, of course, you're going to accuse me of harassment again." His eyes searched her face. "I wouldn't hurt you Jeanette, not for the world."

"I know, John." She grimaced. "When I'm around you, I get all confused," she confessed, ignoring his grin. "And I am not very good at checking."

"You'll catch on, don't worry. Don't be so hard on yourself."

Jeanette studied his face. She'd never seen him serious before. "I owe you an apology." She sipped the lemon-lime drink he opened for her, her heart warming at his kindness and understanding. "I'm sorry."

Taking up his sandwich, he said, "Accepted. Go ahead, dig in to this elegant repast." He indicated their lunch. Shaking her head, Jeanette opened her chips and began to eat. Suddenly, she felt hungry.

At that moment, Josh stuck his head in the door. He held out his cell. "It's boss man."

John took the phone. "Silas? Umm." He fumbled in his pocket for a cell, pulled it on and turned it on. "I'm sorry. Yes, I forgot again. Sorry." He listened a bit, nodded and finally hung up.

Handing Josh his phone, he told him, "Thanks. I forgot to plug mine in."

Josh grinned. "Again."

John groaned. "Yes, again. At least he had your number."

As Josh left with a chuckle, John grimaced. "Your uncle insists I have a cell since I go to the other stores. It also means he can get me any time. Or, at least, he should be able to..."

Jeanette shook her head. "But you don't check the battery."

John plugged in his cell. "Got that right."

"I am taking you Wednesday, aren't I?" he asked.

"Yes, I'd like that," she said, finding within a shyness toward him she hadn't felt before.

John's forecast about her learning curve proved correct. Before another day passed, Jeanette found herself zipping through the groceries with an ease she would not have believed only twenty-four hours earlier. She basked in John's vocal approval and blushed under the almost tender look in his eyes when he complimented her.

The longer she worked, the more Jeanette came to like John, like his quirky sense of humor, his sensitivity to his customers and his genuine faith. In fact, she began looking forward to her Wednesday evenings with John.

Uncle Silas first suggested John share supper with them on Wednesday evenings. "How about it John? From there, you two can go on to church. I know Evelyn enjoys having you young people around the house."

John hesitated, "I wouldn't want to burden your wife, Silas."

He boomed, "She'll love it, I tell you."

The manager turned to Jeanette. "What do you think?"

Smiling, Jeanette took her uncle's arm. "Don't let Uncle Silas fool you, John, into thinking he's the boss. Aunt Evelyn suggested it this morning."

"You found me out," Silas chuckled. "Well, how about it Amory?"

"Jeanette?" John waited for her to reply, something Jeanette found especially endearing. John had a way of making her feel her opinions mattered, something she often didn't feel with Brad. Brad had a way of overwhelming her and sweeping her along with his plans.

"Jeanette, if you don't..."

"Sorry, my mind wondered for a moment." She smiled at John. "Yes, I'd love to have you share supper with us."

From then on after work Wednesday, he took her home where they shared supper with her aunt and uncle before going to the youth meeting. It became a regular part of the week.

The last Wednesday he had taken her out for ice cream after the meeting.

She grimaced. That had not gone at all well, but then she had not then realized how possessive Brad would become in such a short time. It started out so simply.

She smiled up at Brad who swung along side her. Besides seeing each other in history class, Brad made it a point to seek her out on campus. He often walked her to her classes and encouraged her to study with him in the library.

Jeanette's heart raced at the light in his eyes as he gazed down at her, the touch of his hand on her arm. Just the sight of him striding toward her, made her breath start between her lips and her heart beat quicken.

Darilyn shook her head over her. "You are really gone on him, aren't you? Get real, Jeanette. Brad Marsden may date other girls, but as long as Tony Sornborg's in the picture, Brad isn't going to commit himself to anyone else. Trust me on this one. Tony is still very much in the picture. He's been seen with her several times."

Jeanette frowned. "Surely you don't believe that. I don't. Brad is far too nice to play games with me like that. Besides, I don't think he's seeing Tony any longer."

"I think you protest too much," Darilyn answered with a shake of her head. "Mark my words, Brad cares about one thing and one thing only--what will benefit Brad Marsden."

"But he's a Christian, Darilyn. He won't do anything to hurt me." Though she protested, Darilyn's warning seeded doubt in her heart. Brad did seem more than a little reluctant to talk about his faith.

Uncertainly, Jeanette faced her next date with Brad. He noticed it immediately. "What's wrong, Jeanette?" he asked, when after the concert he drove them into the country and parked the car.

Jeanette could hear her parent's admonition against putting herself in a position that might compromise her principles. Jeanette thought rebelliously, *I can handle things. Brad is a gentleman. He said he just wanted to talk, and she had some things she needed to get straight with him. Things she couldn't talk about where others might overhear.*

Finally she stuttered, "Are you serious about me...us, Brad? I mean, I've heard about you and Tony. I don't want to play games, and you do have somewhat of a reputation on campus. I know we're not exclusive or anything, still..." She felt like an idiot.

Taking her cold hand, Brad warmed it with his own. "You mustn't listen to gossip, Jeanette. You're a lovely, if naive, young woman, and, no, I am not playing games with you. I like spending time with you. Surely you know that."

Jeanette persisted. "Are you engaged to Tony Sornborg?"

He grimaced, "Let's just say, our families have planned our futures since we were both in the cradle."

"Then I don't think we should see each other anymore," she managed, though her voice trembled. She knew Brad heard her uncertainty.

He pulled her closer to him. "Then nothing. I'll see who I want to see. I plan my life, Jeanette, no one else. Not my parents, not Tony...no one. Frankly, I'm sick and tired of having other people trying to run my life. It is my life, and I will run it the way I and I alone see fit."

His voice softened. "I'll see who I want to see. I want to keep seeing you."

"What about God? Brad, what part does He play in your life and your decisions?"

"What about Him?" he growled. Lifting her hand, he turned it over and pressed butterfly kisses on her palm.

Jeanette bit her lip. It was difficult to think with Brad kissing her hand and on up her arm. His other arm held her securely to his side. Tugging her hand away, Jeanette struggled to keep focused. "What place does Jesus Christ have in your life? You are a Christian aren't you?" she asked with uncertainty as one of Rev. Connor's sermon flooded into her mind. One verse in particular stuck in her memory, and it worried her with Brad's adamant declaration of running his life his own way.

"Be ye not unequally yoked together with unbelievers: for what fellowship hath righteousness with unrighteousness? and what communion hath light with darkness?" It was in II Corinthians somewhere she recalled. What if Brad wasn't a Christian? But he went to a Christian college?

Brad laughed at the worry on her face. He lowered his voice. "My answer means a lot to you, doesn't it?"

At her nod, he stroked her cheek, bringing a flush to her skin. "Yes, I do believe in God. He is a good God and wants the best for us. Of course, He expects us to do whatever we can to make things happen. Is that good enough for you?" He didn't give her time to answer as he leaned over and his mouth found hers.

Stifling her conscience, Jeanette reveled in the knowledge that Brad Marsden wanted her. But she pulled back with a nervous laugh when he became too ardent. "Brad, Brad. No."

His frown made her quail. "Brad. Please, I think it's time for you to take me home."

He considered for a time before dropping his arms. "I didn't mean to make you afraid. You really are an innocent aren't you?" He smiled then. "I think I like that."

Jeanette let out a breath she didn't know she held. "I'm a Christian," she said simply.

"Yes, yes of course. I admire girls with principle." He reached for the keys. "How about letting me pick you up for church on Sunday? I'd like you to hear our pastor speak."

"But I've been to your youth meetings." She didn't add, she found them less than inspiring.

"Come on," he coaxed, "one Sunday isn't going to hurt."

"Well...." It seemed to mean a lot to Brad.

"Surely, your aunt and uncle wouldn't forbid you to attend another church for once."

"Of course, they wouldn't forbid it. They aren't my parents."

"Good to hear it. You'll go?" He took her silence for a yes. Jeanette let it stand. Somehow, it made no sense to argue over such a small matter. So why did she feel uneasy?

Putting the car in gear, Brad roared out onto the highway. "I think you'll like First Grand. It's the largest church in town, and Rev. Weathersby is a wonderful speaker. He comes from an old Bostonian family, and we are fortunate to have him."

Jeanette wasn't impressed. Rev. Weathersby seemed very full of himself and his sermon was taken more from the daily news than the Bible. The church itself was elegant with large stained glass windows, a grand pipe organ and a ceiling that almost disappeared overhead. It was a lovely church, but it made Jeanette long for the

informality and warmth of her aunt and uncles' church that made her feel so welcome.

Not that she could articulate her feelings to Brad. She didn't want to hurt his feelings, and like he said, it wasn't important how people worshiped, as long as they did.

Then came Wednesday night when Jeanette went with John to Salsby's Ice Cream parlor. With a flourish John opened a menu. "And what dost the lady desire?"

He had been in rare form and in his presence, Jeanette found herself laughing more than she had since her father had his accident. It felt good. Who said Christians couldn't have fun.

She responded in kind. "The lady," she said in her most haughty tone, "would like the most expensive, richest and grandest sundae available."

John bowed. "As you wish, queen of my heart."

For just a moment, Jeanette's heart stopped beating. A moment later, she laughed. Of course, as usual, John only teased. "My servant, are you going to grant my wish?"

He leaned close, a dangerous glint in his eyes. "What is your dearest wish, queen of my heart?"

Melodramatically, she placed one hand over her heart and flung the other into the air. "Oh, that my knight would ride up to claim my heart."

John caught her hand and with great ceremony kissed the school ring that graced her soft hand. "My lady, please let me be your knight. I will climb the highest mountains, swim the deepest seas, bring you the moon, if you will only say you are mine."

Unexpectedly, Jeanette's heart fluttered. For the first time, she considered John as more than a friend. Something in John's gaze quelled her retort. Silently they gazed at each other, John's hand clasping hers across the small round table.

At that moment, Brad walked into the door with several of his friends. Seeing her with John brought a frown to his lips. Blushing furiously, Jeanette snatched her hand away from John.

Coming to their table, Brad regarded John coldly. "John. Jeanette. I thought you were going to church tonight."

"I was. We were. I mean, we did," Jeanette stuttered, blushing more deeply. She resented Brad's implication of impropriety. What right did Brad have thinking she belonged solely to him?

John, had her gratitude, when he broke the tension. "We just stopped by after church for ice cream."

"And other things. I know your type Amory."

John's lips tightened. "Not everyone is like you Brad," he shot back.

A muscle twitched in Brad's cheek. "What does that mean, Amory?"

"Make of it what you will, Brad," John told him calmly, though Jeanette watched anger flash in his eyes. "Besides, you don't own Jeanette. If you please, we would like to order."

Jeanette quailed under Brad's dark glance and was relieved when he took a seat with his friends. Seeing her distress, John ordered four sundae's to go and took her home where they shared a few moments with her aunt and uncle.

"Thank you, John," she told him later at the door. "You were very kind to think of Uncle Silas and Aunt Evelyn. About Brad?"

He put a finger to her lips. "Queen of my heart, you have no need to make apologies."

As he left, Jeanette touched her lips. They burned with John's light touch as though he'd kissed her.

She thought no more of Brad until the next afternoon.

CHAPTER SEVEN:

The next afternoon, Brad accosted her as she hurried
toward her tailoring class. On her mind was how she
was going to solve the problem with the formal gown
she was making for the class. The project served a
double purpose, for it was the gown she planned to wear
in July as Sandie's maid of honor. Somehow, she just
couldn't get the lace bodice to turn quite right.

"Jeanette, wait!" Hurrying to catch up with her, Brad
grabbed the sleeve of her coat.

"Brad, what is it? I've got a class." Jeanette tried to
keep her irritation from her tone.

"I need to talk to you."

Though the day was rather warm for March, she
shivered at the coldness in Brad's eyes. "I can't right
now. If it's about last night," she started. "I don't want
to talk about it. Later." Much later, she thought.

"Look Jeanette, I'm sorry if I embarrassed you, but I
do need to talk with you." Deliberately, Jeanette glanced
at her watch. Brad took the hint. "All right. All right, I'll
let you go to your class. But, we do need to talk. When
is your next free period?"

Jeanette shifted her bookbag to her other shoulder.
"I'm not free until twelve...at the earliest."

"Lunch then." It was more a statement than a question. Letting that irritating habit of his slide, Jeanette nodded.

"I'll pick you up."

Promptly at twelve, Brad picked her up in his car and drove her to a nearby restaurant. Though the place was crowded, they managed to find a table in a relatively quite corner by a picture window that looked out toward City Park.

"Pretty soon the leaves will start coming on and the grass will green," Jeanette commented staring out the window. "I'll bet the park is pretty in the summer."

Brad pointed toward the white marble basin with a cupid rising from it. "Once the frost is gone, they turn on the water and cupid spouts water into the basin. By the summer, the walkway around the basin is bright with every kind and color of flowers." Leaning back in his seat, he smiled at her. "I hope to show it to you."

"What if I return home for the summer?"

"I'll have to lure you back," he said. "Why go home at all? Other than for a short visit."

He stopped as a harried waitress asked for their order that she wrote down on her pad before hurrying away.

"I don't envy her job," Jeanette said. "I had enough trouble learning my job at uncle's store." With an inward grimace, she recalled how she easy she thought such work would be. Once she'd started working at the store, she realized how difficult any job could be. "John's been very patient with me. More than I deserve."

"Not without his own reasons." Brad frowned at the mention of the name. "That's what I wanted to talk to you about."

"My job? I don't think that concerns you."

"No, but John does. About last night...."

He stopped again and waited impatiently as the waitress set down their drinks. He sipped his root beer before continuing. "I thought John's behavior last evening was inappropriate, yours too, for that matter."

Jeanette's eyes narrowed. "We were just having a little fun. What's wrong with going out for ice cream after youth group? It's not as though you and I are engaged or anything."

"But you and I are dating."

"So are John and I. You know that. We go to church together and out to lunch once and a while. Haven't you been seeing Tony?"

"That's different; we've been friends for years."

"That's just it. People see you two together and wonder about us. You should hear Darilyn on the subject."

Brad grimaced, "I'd rather not. Tony and I are friends. You'll have to accept my word on that." He reached for her hand, only to once more be interrupted as the waitress plopped baskets, containing chicken and fries, in front of each of them.

After the waitress moved on, he said, "What I am trying to say is that I wish you would not go out with John."

Jeanette took a bite of chicken and washed it down with her lemon-lime pop. "Are you jealous?" The thought rather appealed to her.

"I just don't think Amory is the sort of person you should be hanging around with."

Jeanette's eyes flashed. She always found it easier to defend others than herself. "Just why not," she asked with deadly calm.

"You don't need to get angry. John is a nice enough fellow, but he works in a grocery store, after all. Where's that going to get him in life?"

"John is the manager, and Uncle Silas thinks very highly of him. Besides, I also work in a grocery story, and you forget who owns that very same store."

A muscle in his left cheek twitched. "That's my point. Your uncle has made something of himself. He owns that store, and others. He's a real businessman, but it's been a struggle for him financially and otherwise.

"Tell me, where would John get capital for a business venture...if he had the ambition." He paused before continuing, "As for you, working at the store is only temporary. It's admirable to want to earn your way. I admire that."

Jeanette gripped her glass. The sun caught the stone on her class ring and flashed into her eyes, reminding her vividly of the sacrifice her parents made just so she could have the ring. It was a sacrifice she had not understood until she took over the farm work and tried to balance the farm budget.

"Admire? Want to earn my way? Brad, I have to work. I've explained all this to you before. My folks may live on a farm that has been in our family for several generations, but we are not rich. We're not even close, especially since Dad's accident. If I didn't work, I wouldn't be going to ProMark. Now if you can't accept who I am, then...."

Brad grabbed her hand. "Calm down, Jeanette, others are looking at us."

Jeanette flushed and stared down at the table, up at Brad. The sun set off his blond hair in a halo. "I'm sorry Brad, but sometimes you make me feel like I'm not good enough for you. John never makes me feel small like you do sometimes."

Scowling, Brad squeezed her hand so hard she tugged it away. "John again," he grated. With difficulty, he calmed himself. "Listen, Jeanette, it doesn't matter about the family income, not really. It's more than that. What does matter is that your folks are solid respectable people. I know that, because I know their daughter." He smiled his devastating smile, but it didn't ease Jeanette's frown.

"I may even be in love with their daughter." A look she wasn't sure how to interpret flashed in his eyes. "Why else would I want to be alone with you, to hold you and kiss those lovely red lips?"

"Shh." A guilty stain spread across her cheeks as thoughts of the times she'd allowed him to park alongside a deserted road and do just that, flashed in her mind.

Brad chuckled softly. "You've done nothing to be ashamed of my little puritan--yet."

Jeanette cocked her head, listening, unsure what to think. When she remained silent, Brad continued, "I'd rather you not date anyone else, including John. After all, he has no plans to better himself with education. As for his mother, she used to work for us you know. As for his father... I'm sure John would rather everyone forgot about him."

The flush of Brad's endearment was lost in his condescending remarks about John. Taking the last fry, Jeanette ate it with slow deliberation, took another sip of her pop and slowly got to her feet. "Brad Marsden," she said firmly, "I never heard such prejudice in my life. John has to work to help support his mother. You well know she is in ill health. Further, I know how hard he works at the store.

"As for dating him, until now I hadn't even considered it all that seriously, but you don't own me Brad Marsden, and you will certainly not tell me whether or not to be friends with John." Head high, she marched from the restaurant. Half way to the street she stopped in consternation, realizing she had come with Brad and had no other way back to the campus.

She hesitated, wondering if she could catch a ride with someone else back to the campus. If she had to, she'd walk. Not the best alternative since that would make her late for her next class. Seeing little choice, Jeanette settled the strap of her purse more firmly onto her shoulder and prepared to cross the street. Honk!

Startled she jumped back, glaring at Brad as he slid to a stop in front of her and opened the passenger door.

"Look Jeanette, I'm sorry. I know you need to get back."

"I can walk," she told him, wishing the light breeze wouldn't ruffle his hair in such an appealing fashion.

"What will you do for books?" He held up her backpack stuffed with books and papers.

Sighing, she slid into the seat. With a sidelong glance at her rigid features, he turned the key. On campus, she opened the door and stepped out. "Thank you for lunch, Brad. It was....revealing."

She frowned when he merely grinned. "Very good."

"What's so funny?"

"My Jeanette," he began only to have her interrupt.

"I'm not your Jeanette. I'm not anyone's Jeanette."

He raised a hand. "You've got old fashion spunk. I like that. Good material to work with. Frankly, Jeanette Roberts, I've never known any girl in which I've shown an interest to be so hard to win over."

"Right, Brad Marsden. I get it. I'm nothing but a challenge to you. Well, this girl isn't interested, thank you." With that, she swung around and headed toward class. At the door, she turned to find Brad staring after her, determination written all over his face.

Jeanette managed to get through the rest of her classes as well as to avoid Darilyn's questions. At the store after classes, she ran the register with scarce a thought, and she let her mind wander as she ran one item after another over the price scanner.

She had begun the year with such high hopes. That was before she met Brad. He was so assured, so handsome and his kisses were both passionate and exciting. Jeanette wished he hadn't reminded her of the times she allowed him to drive her out into the country. She excused herself with, "We mostly talked." Yet her conscience continued to bother her.

It was all over now. After the scene in the restaurant, then on campus, Brad would never forgive her. But she had to stand up for John. Why, she wasn't sure. It wasn't as though there was anything serious between them. Nonetheless, she couldn't deny she enjoyed being with John. His teasing smile, that once so irritated her, brought a sense of joy.

She fumbled, and jammed the register. With an embarrassed laugh, she picked up the phone. "John to check out #4, please."

He found her trying to apologize to the same businessman who had been so impatient with her that first week. Having been in several times since then, the man was more patient, but Jeanette was thankful when John once more smoothed things over.

That evening after work when John held her coat while she slipped it on, he asked, "How about a movie tonight?"

"I didn't see anything playing downtown I'd like to see," she said slowly.

"I agree," John said. "I thought maybe you wouldn't mind renting a movie. We can have dinner with Mom, then watch the movie..." he prosed, "with all the comforts of home. I might even be able to manage sundaes for the lady." Kneeling, he raised his arms, "Please say you'll come, Queen of my heart."

Giggling, Jeanette stared down her nose at him. "Let me thumb through my appoint book. Let's see. Hmm. I guess I could squeeze you in. Yikes!" Suddenly, she found herself waltzing down the aisle with John. "Stop. Stop!" She cried as they nearly bumped into a display she'd set up but a couple hours earlier.

Panting, she tried to catch her breath as he swung her about and lifted her onto the check out counter. "Your enthusiasm overwhelms. Do you ever have second dates?" she asked.

He merely laughed. Later, in his beat up pickup, she realized she'd agreed to spend the evening with John without a second thought as to what Brad would think. What's more, she didn't care. And they had a wonderful time.

The next Saturday, John rescheduled to give them both the day off. Since the sun beamed down warm and bright, Jeanette carried her coat over her arm as she walked outside.

She surveyed the old, but serviceable car. "Where's the pickup?"

"Thought I'd impress you with the latest sportscar. How do you like it? It has all the features--a steering wheel, tires and an engine that runs. Afraid I can't claim

that right now about the pickup." He sighed and Jeanette sensed an undertone of dejection.

"In the shop again?"

"'fraid so. This is Mom's car, though she seldom drives." He opened the door. "My lady."

John gave Jeanette, dressed in jade slacks and matching V-necked top she both designed and sewed herself, a low whistle as he settled her into his mother's car.

"Nice threads. You didn't get those on a grocery clerk's budget."

"Thanks. And thanks again."

"What's the second thanks for?"

"For the compliment."

Laughter bubbled up inside at his puzzled glance. Smoothing down her slacks, she told him rather shyly, "I designed and sewed this outfit."

She thrilled to his low whistle of appreciation. "I am impressed." He looked her up and down until she blushed.

He asked, "Designed, too?" She nodded. "You have talent."

Her heart sang at his genuine praise. "Thank you." Embarrassed under his effusive compliments, she changed the subject as she buckled her seat belt. "Where we headed?"

"Have you ever been to Lindsborg, the Swedish village?" he asked as he headed the car onto 135 north. He squinted against the bright sun, glinting off the still icy roads.

"No, I haven't, at least I don't think so. I'm afraid, we hardly ever went anywhere. Mother talked about the town, but, if I ever went, it was when I was too young to remember. My mother is Swedish, a Fredrickson," she explained. "She made me proud of being Swedish. In fact, I always wanted to know more about my Swedish heritage."

"With those blue eyes of yours, I rather guessed there might be a bit of Swedish in your background." John grinned. "Anyhow, that's where we're headed."

Jeanette clapped her hands. "Thank you John, how did you know? Have you a Swedish background?"

He turned his dark eyes on her. "Not exactly. Not at all in fact. Afraid I'm German clear through. But then I wish to please my little Swedish lass."

His mocking Swedish brogue earned him a cuff on the arm as Jeanette settled back in her seat. "So I've gone from Queen to a mere lass."

"Ah, my pretty, thou canst be both." Jeanette blushed under the tender light in his eyes and turned away.

As though sensing her discomfort, John kept the conversation light. Before long, Jeanette found herself responding to him comfortably; laughing and talking and revealing more of herself than she had to anyone else in a long time.

Before she knew, it they reached Lindsborg, and John was helping her from the car. Taking her hand, he led her down the sidewalk. "What shall we see first?"

Spinning around, she exclaimed, "Oh everything."

Laughing, John's hand caught hers. "Just for today, let's pretend."

"Pretend what?"

"That we're more than friends."

When she hesitated, he laughed, but it seemed rather forced. "Forget it."

"No. No. I like the idea. Just for today."

"Yes, for today." John held her close for a moment, but released her before she could push away. Strangely enough, she wasn't sure she wanted to.

Along with the few tourists, for it was not yet the tourist season, Jeanette and John, hand in hand, meandered through the quaint Swedish shops. They watched as a man in a leather apron cut the little Swedish horses, and watched them being painted in the traditional colors of red-orange, blue and yellow.

In the window of one shop John pointed out a notice of the Svensk Hyllningsfest the second week in October. "How about it, Jeanette, shall we make it a date?"

"I'd love to," Jeanette agreed, "but that's almost six months away. I doubt you'll remember."

"Ah, lass, I have an amazing memory."

John treated her to authentic Svenska Peppar Kakor and Fattigman, and at noon they heaped their plates at a local smorgasbord.

Clouds drifted across the warm sun as John pulled her down beside him on one of many narrow benches along the buildings. Drowsily, she leaned her head against his shoulder, feeling a sense of security and well being. John patted his middle and groaned. "I haven't eaten so much, in months."

Jeanette raised her head, a smile lingering on her lips. Leaning down, John touched his lips to hers in a kiss so tender, Jeanette melted against him.

A rumble rolled over them, but, caught up with each other, neither noticed. The clouds scuttled across the sun, dark and threatening. Wind whipped down the street chasing dead leaves, twigs, paper and a hat or two. Just as suddenly, the clouds growled and rain plopped ever more quickly onto the sidewalk.

Releasing her, John pulled Jeanette to her feet. "Come on," he cried, wrapping his arm around her. John shielded her as best he could as they ran for the car. Rain pelted down on them as he slammed the door.

Breathing heavily, they stared at each other. Both had lived in Kansas all their lives and understood the danger of a late winter storm.

Quickly putting the car in gear, John glanced toward Jeanette. "I think we can make it home, unless you don't want to try."

"Let's go," Jeanette said, buttoning up her coat against the cold that penetrated the chilled car.

With a nod, John headed out of town. The furnace kicked in for which Jeanette gave silent thanks. She watched as John flipped on the windshield wipers that vainly tried to clear the torrent of rain from the glass, rain mingled with heavy snow. Once on the highway, he turned on the radio.

"High winds. Rain turning to snow and ice." John's lips tightened. "We'll make it home," he ground out. A couple minutes later, he whispered, "Pray, Jeanette. We're going to need it if we're going to stay safe." She heard him mutter, "My cell." Reaching into his pocket, he pulled out a phone and turned it on. It emitted a sick sounding beap and died. He shook it and put it on the dash. I forgot to charge it—as usual. He grunted his disgust at himself.

"Do you have a cell?"

She pulled out hers and clicked. "Not much reception here."

He groaned.

Five miles from town the car skidded on the slick rain turned to ice. Jeanette clutched John's arm as he gripped the wheel. There was nothing he could do. With a thud, the car hit a guardrail and careened down the embankment into the ditch.

CHAPTER EIGHT

"Lord, help us! Protect us," Jeanette whispered. She felt herself hurling forward and then a hard thump.

From far away, she heard John's voice edged in concerned. "Jeanette. Jeanette are you all right?" She felt his arm stretch across her, heard him grunt as he tried to release her seatbelt. Heard the sharp snap as he forced it open and felt herself falling. "John!"

Wrapping his arms about her, John pulled her close. "It's all right, Jeanette. God answered your prayer. We're all right. For now," he muttered under his breath. For a moment, wind lifted the curtain of snow to reveal their desperate situation. The car tilted downward at a steep angle in the deep roadside ditch.

Shaking, Jeanette buried her head against John's warm shoulder. He held her close, murmuring soothingly until she calmed. Taking a deep breath, she straightened. "Oh John, what happened!" she cried, seeing the blood staining his coat. "You're hurt!" She swayed dizzily, glad for John's protecting arm.

"I'm fine. Jeanette." John was tying to remain calm, but Jeanette heard the ragged edge to his tone. "You're hurt. Your forehead."

Gingerly, Jeanette touched her forehead. Her shaking hand came away sticky with blood. "Oh." Again she swayed and tried to focus her eyes.

"Lean back," John commanded. He tried to force open the glove compartment for the first aid kit his mother always kept handy; grunted when the glove compartment door refused to open. Jeanette's pale face and glazed eyes scared him. Struggling out of his coat and sweater, John removed his shirt. Ripping off a sleeve, he wrapped it about Jeanette's head. She watched it all, as though feeling detached--floating.

Her soft smile frightened him most of all. He had to get her to a hospital. "I'm going to try to get a look around," he told her, reaching for the door handle.

The door wouldn't budge. He tried again. He even considered breaking a window, but the snow still fell, and there was no telling where or if there was other shelter nearby. If only he hadn't tried to drive home.

Turning around with some difficulty, John managed to open a back window. It wasn't large, but still he tried to squeeze his large frame through it. He got stuck half way out.

"Jeanette, can you help pull me back," he yelled, his words muffled by snow and wind. Reaching over, he rubbed the snow from another window and peered in at his companion. "Jeanette, help me."

He watched her shake her head and bite her lip as though in concentration. "Jeanette. Grab my belt and pull."

Slowly, she reached back and grabbed his belt. "That's it. Now pull. Good. Keep it up." With her assistance, John squirmed back inside the car and rolled the window back up, but not before snow blew into the car, covering everything inside with a shower of stinging icy snow.

Jeanette leaned back against the seat, her eyes closed. For a moment, John rested his head in his hands. "Lord," he groaned. "Jeanette needs help, and there is nothing I can do. Please send help."

Her head thumped against him, and he glanced down at her quiet face. Too quiet. He felt her forehead. It was clammy. "Jeanette. Jeanette. Wake up. Wake up!" From somewhere came the knowledge that he must keep her awake.

Jeanette smiled at him through soft dazed eyes. "What's your name?" he yelled at her. When she didn't respond he called even louder, "What's your name?"

"Don't...have...to yell." She frowned as though thinking hurt her head.

He enunciated slowly and clearly. "What is your name?"

"J...Jeanette Roberts," she said finally to John's immense relief.

"Jeanette, we're stuck here, and you need help. We have to pray for someone to find us."

She nodded. Grimaced as the movement hurt her neck and head. Holding her close, John wrapped his coat about them both and bowed his head.

Jeanette, listening to him pray, was humbled at the depth of John's faith, and his obvious concern for her. Her heart warmed within her. Her last rational thought was that her parents would really like John.

"Miss Roberts. Jeanette." The voice coaxed her from a safe haven far away. "Jeanette, can you hear me."

Slowly focusing her eyes, Jeanette stared up at the white-coated doctor, for he could be nothing else, leaning over her. The man's ruffled hair was an uncertain shade of brownish-red with a sprinkling of gray at the temples. The strong chin and gray eyes studied her with penetrating clarity.

"Where...?" Coughing, she licked her lips. A nurse at the doctor's elbow held a glass of water for her. After a long slow sip, she tried again. "Where am I?"

"You're at McFadden Memorial Hospital where your young man brought you after the accident."

The memory flashed through her mind. "How...how? Where? Is John all right?"

The doctor smiled at her. "Frostbite, but otherwise yes. As for you. You have a concussion, young lady, and I'm afraid we'll have to keep you here for observation for a couple of days."

Feeling the tight bandage about her head, Jeanette listened to his admonishments and his directions to the nurse with only half her attention. What happened? How had she gotten here? Was John really all right?

Distracted, she perked up when the doctor opened the door to her aunt and uncle, who hurried into the room, worry written on their faces.

"Oh, Jeanette." Her aunt smoothed back the hair straggling over her shoulder. "Are you all right? My dear. I would never forgive myself if something happened to you."

Her uncle stood on the other side of the bed. He carried a vase filled with pink roses and baby's breath that he set on the stand beside her bed. "How are you feeling?" She winced at his booming voice.

"John. Is he really all right?" Jeanette tried to sit up, but Aunt Evelyn restrained her with firm, but gentle hands.

Silas chuckled. "You have much for which to thank that young man. He saved your life."

Jeanette turned questioning eyes toward her aunt who nodded. "When you didn't return we got worried. We called John's mother hoping you'd made it to their house, but found she hadn't heard from John. She was frantic with worry."

"So was your Aunt Evelyn," Silas continued. "Your aunt called every motel and inn near Lindsborg, they were full of stranded people, but no one had checked in with your names. We realized then you must have gotten caught in the storm on your way home. "

Evelyn smiled at her husband, her eyes soft with love. "That's when Silas notified the police you were missing. As soon as the wind let up, he went out to find you."

"Uncle, thank you, but John?"

"Don't thank me. John somehow managed to open the back door, lift you up out of the car and carry you to the road where we found you. By that time, the car was completely covered up with snow. If he hadn't gotten you out when he did..." Silas shook his head. "How he managed is a miracle. But you're here and you're safe. Thank God."

"And John?" Jeanette insisted, her head beginning to throb.

"He's fine," Aunt Evelyn told her. "Don't you worry about him."

Entering the room, a nurse asked them to leave. As glad as she was to see them, Jeanette was tired and ready to end their visit. When she awoke again, the room was dark, and, for the first time, she wondered how long she had been in the hospital. A night nurse came at her buzzer and seemed irritated at her question. "How long have I been here?"

Checking the chart, she said, "They brought you in yesterday afternoon. Concussion. Don't you recall us waking you up every two hours last night?"

Jeanette shook her head. "What day is it?"

"Monday night." The hefty nurse glanced at her watch. "No Tuesday morning."

Monday. What about school? Work? Her head began to pound again. She was so tired. Moments after the nurse closed her door, Jeanette was again fast asleep.

The next morning, Jeanette awoke clear headed and alert. The shades had already been opened, and she looked out the tall window over a wide expanse of white, slit by a ribbon of road. Sitting up, she was about to slide to the floor when the door opened admitting the doctor. "Ah, I see we're feeling better this morning."

Jeanette returned his smile. "May I go home today?"

"We'll see," he said as he unwound the bandage from her head and prodded the wound until Jeanette winced. He left it for his nurse to tend and re-bandage.

After writing on the chart in his hand, the doctor studied her carefully. "Are you sure you feel up to going home?"

"Yes, please. I want to go home."

"To your aunt and uncle? Not all the way home." He smiled.

Jeanette nodded slowly to keep her headache from returning. "I see no reason why not," he said, "you seem to being doing fine. But," he said with a decided frown, "you must take it easy the next couple of days."

"I have school and work..."

"Not until I see you again Thursday."

Jeanette slumped against the pillows. She really didn't feel well, but was concerned about getting behind in school and not earning her way.

Uncle Silas came for her just before lunch and took her home where Aunt Evelyn fed and pampered her until Jeanette protested. "Please, you're both doing much too much. I need to get up. I really should go to the store with you Uncle Silas."

"No. Now don't worry about a thing. I told your folks we'd take good care of you, and we plan to do just that."

"You called them?"

"Of course," her Aunt said. "They were all set to drive down, but we told them you were coming along fine."

Her uncle boomed, "We certainly didn't want your folks out in this weather."

"I'm glad you convinced them to stay home." Jeanette smiled, but found even a smile hurt. "May I call them?"

Silas brought her a cordless phone. After assuring her parents she was back with her aunt and uncle, and being properly pampered, she hung up.

"About my things?"

Her asked, "From the car?" Jeanette nodded.

"Silas will go out and retrieve the car once the weather permits." Biting her lip, Jeanette nodded again. This time in relief.

Jeanette found, that despite her protests, she had exhausted her meager resources and thankfully slid under the covers. She slept most of the afternoon, awaking to a darkening room.

Slowly, she reached over and flipped on the lamp beside her bed. The light hurt her eyes, and she turned away to let them adjust to the light. Swinging her feet over the side of the bed, she gingerly got to her feet. She steadied herself against the wall, and waited until the room stopped spinning before carefully making her way to the bathroom.

With every small step, she found herself getting stronger. Once back in her room, she slipped on comfortable sweats. Though her aunt wanted to bring her supper to her on a tray, Jeanette insisted on joining them in the dining room.

Afterward, she curled up in the large wing back chair by the fireplace, trying to catch up on her school work. Darilyn dropped by with the assignments when she was sleeping, and her aunt refused to wake her. Her headache began again, and she set aside the heavy history textbook.

At that moment, the doorbell buzzed. Uncle Silas had gone to the store and her Aunt, after Jeanette insisted, left to attend her Women's Bible Study. With a groan, Jeanette pushed herself to her feet. When she didn't answer immediately, the door opened, and John strode into the room. He looked relieved to see her standing. Angry, too. "What are you doing up? Of course, the door." Picking her up, he set her back into the chair. She liked the feel of his arms around her and felt bereft when he released her.

"Silas said I could check on you. When you didn't answer the door, I got worried." He surveyed her comfortable worn sweats, a smile tickling his lips.

His amusement irritated her. "I'm comfortable."

"Of course." He sat down opposite her on the wide couch. "Are you really all right?"

Her irritation faded. "Thank you for what you did. I heard you saved my life."

He turned his head to hide the flush on his cheeks. "Your uncle told you."

"You were very brave, John." Reaching out, she touched his arm. Warmth oozed up her arm and right down to her toes. Touching him had been a mistake, and she let her hand fall to her side.

"I care about you, Jeanette." His sober look faded into a teasing grin, "I certainly couldn't have you bleeding all over Mom's car."

Jeanette stared into the flame of the fireplace. There was so much she liked about John, but his teasing sometimes still irritated her. It was almost as though he was afraid of becoming too serious--about any thing. She wished he would stay serious long enough to let her really know how he felt about her. She thought, with a blush, of being held in his strong arms.

He snapped his fingers, "Jeanette, are you with me." His eyes had grown serious again. "You are all right?"

"Sorry. No, I'm fine, John, just thinking."

He touched the bandage and, with surprising gentleness, traced the curve of her cheek. "If you're sure?"

At her nod, he sat back and surveyed her quietly. "This may not be the best of time, Jeanette, but there is something I meant to talk to you about."

He was serious again, and Jeanette briefly closed her eyes. Was he finally going to talk about their relationship? Was there one, other than friendship? Her heart racing with hope, Jeanette sat forward. "What is it, John?"

More uneasy than she'd ever seen him, John got up and strode around the room before sitting down on the chair's edge again. "Jeanette, there's been talk." Letting out a long breath, he hurried on as though determined to get out what was on his mind. "Brad has been seen parking on some rather notorious country roads with a girl."

Jeanette clenched her teeth in an attempt to keep her cheeks from giving her away. How could anyone have found out?

John continued. "I'm not accusing you of anything, Jeanette, but I think you know parking is not something geared to help a girl maintain a blameless image, especially a Christian image. God calls us to a higher standard. And Brad...well, he does have a certain reputation."

Her eyes flashing, Jeanette burst out, "How dare you make such accusations. Brad has been very kind to me, and we just talked." She knew she gave herself away. The disappointment in John's eyes made her feel unclean.

At John's penetrating gaze, she gulped, "We just talked. Well, almost. Honest. We didn't do anything wrong. I didn't," she conceded, wondering why she felt obligated to tell John anything at all. She sensed she'd hurt him.

Staring into the fireplace, she waited, for what? What was there to say in her defense? Silence. A log burned through and crashed, sending sparks up the chimney.

Finally, John spoke. "I hoped I was wrong, Jeanette. Do you care about Brad so much?"

Glancing at him, Jeanette was surprised at the pain in his eyes. Did he care about her? "I don't know," she said honestly. "It doesn't much matter. Brad and I are finished. We don't view things the same way." She didn't explain further. "Why? Do you care?" She asked, feeling the heat in her cheeks at her question.

John sat back, a smile once more on his lips. Ignoring her last questions he responded, "I'm glad to hear you and Brad have gone your separate ways. Tony Sornborg has Brad at her beck and call and I didn't want you hurt. Besides, your uncle asked me to watch out for you."

Jeanette's cheeks flamed with an embarrassment she could not explain. John only cared because of Uncle Silas. That hurt. Jeanette forced it away. She had been foolish to hope, and John hadn't ever given her any reason to think otherwise.

Seeming to realize, he had hurt her in some way, John extended himself to cheer her up. His quirky stories and humor had her laughing, and when he left an hour later, Jeanette had to admit she felt better.

Settling down to sleep later that night, Jeanette thought over her evening. It had taken courage for John to confront her about her behavior with Brad. It wouldn't happen again, IF Brad ever asked her out again. She thought about Brad's broad shoulders and devastating smile. A seductive smile, she thought drowsily as her eyes closed.

As though her thoughts conjured him up, Jeanette found Brad knocking at her door the next morning. Seeing his handsome face made her heart race. Brad had come to see her!

CHAPTER NINE:

Silas had already left for a business meeting with his
store managers when Evelyn admitted Brad and
motioned him toward Jeanette, who sat hunched over
her books spread out on the dining room table.

Dressed in casual cream slacks and blue ski sweater,
Jeanette wrote furiously, determined to keep up with her
class. She made a commitment not only to attend school,
but to do well enough to keep her scholarships. Before
Darilyn's first class, Jeanette called her for the latest
assignments in the classes they shared. Another call to
her teachers got her other assignments.

On the counter, Evelyn had her small kitchen
television on low as she cleaned up from breakfast. She
left it on as she went downstairs to start a load of wash.

"Jeanette." Brad set a single long-stemmed red rose
in a delicate cut crystal vase beside her on the table.
"I've been concerned about you. If only you hadn't..."

Jeanette raised her hand to restrain the comment. "If
you're going to talk about my friendship with John, you
might as well leave. John probably saved my life."

Brad took a chair beside her. "And you're grateful,
but he shouldn't have started back to McFadden in that
storm."

"It was as much my decision as his," Jeanette told him. "Besides, it wasn't all that bad when we started, and we thought we could make it back. If it was a mistake in judgment, the blame is as much mine as his. If you don't mind, I have a lot of work to catch up on."

Leaning over, he caught the title of her paper. "Another paper for Miss Tornbloom," he said with a grimace. "Talk about slave driver. I suppose she wouldn't give you any extra time."

Jeanette shook her head. "It's all right, I rather enjoy research." She offered her paper. "Harriet Tubman was quite the woman. She did what she believed was right, no matter what. She brought out hundreds of slaves, worked as both nurse and spy during the civil war and opened her home to many needy people after the war."

Handing back the report, Brad waited until she finished. "I'm glad you're done. Is there anything else I could help you with?"

"No, I'm managing." Jeanette did not wish to hurt his feelings, but she always studied and prepared better alone. "Thank you for the rose. It's lovely." She fingered a delicate petal.

Brad cleared his throat. "Jeanette, about the other day."

"Other day?" Her eyebrows rose. "It's been almost two weeks ago, Brad."

"Yes, well, I've been rather busy." She waited, not intending to make this easy for him. "Jeanette, if you want an apology, you have it. I was out of line." He took her hand.

"It's just that I was beginning to feel a proprietary interest in you, and I didn't want you with John--or anyone else."

Her hand burned in his. "Brad, Darilyn has seen you out with Tony."

"Social obligations." He lowered his voice, "If you were mine, it would be you at those functions with me. Think of it, balls, receptions; meeting dignitaries and politicians. You'd like that wouldn't you?" It wasn't a question.

When she hesitated, he coaxed. "Jeanette, I want you back."

He pulled her close, and she melted under the warmth of his gaze. Like a bell, John's warning rang in her mind, and she straightened. "If we do get back together," she said, pausing at what she contemplated, "and I do mean if, things have to be different."

"Different. In what way?"

She resented the light of victory in his eyes, but stilled her irritation. "At no time will I park on the country roads with you again." Her cheeks bloomed with color. "Or any other place."

"I see. Are you afraid? Or has your friend John said something against me?"

Her blush gave him the answer. "Who I spoke with isn't important. You and I both know that as Christians we have certain standards and parking doesn't match those standards."

Brad commented dryly, "Old fashioned maybe."

Jeanette interrupted with a frown. "No God's standards of right and wrong are for our protection and our good. I was wrong in...in what I allowed. Whatever your other dates have done, I won't do it--not again."

"All right. I respect that," Brad told her. "That said, how about going out with me Friday night?"

"I don't know." She touched her forehead, feeling a headache coming on. "The doctor...."

Brad interrupted, "If the doctor approves?"

Shaking her head slowly at his determination, she left him hanging with a simple, "We'll see."

Suddenly, a familiar voice caught her attention. She glanced up in surprise to see her sister gyrating seductively about the small television screen, holding a bottle of some alcoholic beverage. Her face pale, Jeanette watched as Cynthia, dressed in not much, encouraged the viewer to purchase the drink. "She's selling alcohol. How could she do that?" Brad misinterpreted her anguished cry.

"I know you don't approve, Jeanette, but selling is a business after all." She scarcely heard Brad's comment. Jumping up, she shut the television off with a snap. So that was Cynthia's commercial, the commercial Jeanette hoped would be the beginning of good things for her sister. She felt sick.

That evening, John brought over a pizza for supper. As she helped him lay out the pizza on paper plates and pour the root beer, she told him. "I'm not going to Paul's Marks tonight, you know. Afraid I'm not up to a night out with the crowd yet."

With a mischievous grin, John patted her cheek. "Yes, my lass, I'm well aware of that." He picked up two of the plates and returned them to the stack in the cupboard.

"Hay, what are you doing?" Jeanette headed back toward the cupboard. Catching her around the waist, John hauled her back.

For a moment, he held her close, released her as he chuckled, "There's just going to be the two of us?"

"Why didn't Aunt Evelyn tell me? Where are they?"

"Your Uncle is taking your Aunt to dinner. He thought she needed a break, and we thought you'd like the surprise."

Jeanette checked the clock. She had been concerned that her aunt and uncle would be late for their prayer meeting, now her concern was for John. "You'll be late, you know."

Holding a chair for her, he smiled as she sat down. "I'm staying right here with you this evening. There is a couple of movies we can watch if you like, or I can just sit and drink in your loveliness." With a deep sigh, he opened his eyes and ogled her until she chortled.

"John, get your elbow out of the pizza."

His woebegone expression draw her giggle as he wiped off his sleeve. "Oh the trials of love."

Jeanette shook her head at him. Taking her hand, John held it as he blessed the food.

"This is delicious," Jeanette said sometime later, "but I've had my fill. What about you?"

He eyed the three pieces still in the box. "Unfortunately, yes. Maybe we could heat them up for snack later."

She laughed as she covered the rest of the pizza and placed it into the frig, while John cleaned up the table, doing a perfect imitation, whether he realized it or not, of the starched waiter at the restaurant Brad took her to in Hutchinson.

Afterward he guided her downstairs, rather as though fearing she might fall, to the family room and ensconced her in a low rust-colored couch facing the large screen television set. Continuing his role, he bowed and presented his choices. "Let's see, the latest Christian comedian or a chick-flick? Guaranteed to make you cry."

Jeanette chose the comedian. She blushed lightly when John sat down beside her and put his arm about her shoulders. He coiled a long strand of her hair around his finger. "I like your beautiful long hair down around your shoulders." His husky undertone surprised her. Did she think John getting serious bothered him? She found it equally a problem for her.

Not quite knowing how to handle the situation, she quipped, "You said sitting in a parked car was dangerous."

A look flashed across his face she did not understand, and he dropped his arm. She stuttered, "I...I didn't mean to hurt your feelings."

"No you're right, Jeanette," he said with unusual seriousness. "You are entirely too tempting."

She didn't know what to make of that and wondered about it during the show.

Afterward she asked, "Your mother's car. Did you get it out of the ditch?"

"Thanks to Uncle Silas. We pulled it out late yesterday. The mechanic says it suffered relatively minor damage. Thank the Lord. I wouldn't want Mom to be without transportation, and she can't handle my rig."

"I'm glad it turned out all right. You do have your pickup back, don't you?"

"I do now. Silas let me use one of his vehicles until I got it back. You're uncle is a pretty special person."

"I know. He and Aunt Evelyn spoil me rotten. But if you got the car back, where are my things?"

"Ask your uncle. He probably forgot to bring them home." After a moment, John drawled, "I heard Brad dropped by."

Jeanette tensed. "He wanted to know how I was." When John didn't say anything, she blurted, "I talked to him about--you know. I won't do it again."

Though she wasn't sure why she told John, and it really didn't concern him, the joy in his eyes at the news, amply repaid her. "I'm glad. I was afraid you'd never speak to me again when I confronted you."

Glancing at him, then away, Jeanette whispered, "Thank you for caring enough to speak to me about it." She bit her lip. "I guess I needed to see how it looked to others. Brad, well, he's very persuasive. No," she said, "I know I'm as much to blame. But I told him that if we ever went out again, that was not to be part of the evening."

"Good for you." He took her hands in his. "Never sell yourself short, Jeanette. Not for anyone."

When her aunt and uncle returned they were back upstairs raiding the freezer for ice cream. John dished some up for them as well.

When he left, her uncle all but smirked. "Have a nice evening?"

"Uncle Silas, stop playing matchmaker. I do like John, but we're just friends. Just friends." Why did she sound so disappointed?

"Hmm." was all her uncle said, but the intensity of his gaze brought a flush to her cheeks.

She changed the subject. "About my things from John's car?"

Her uncle actually hit his forehead with his palm. "I forgot. Your bag and cell are in the car." Getting up, he went to get them.

"Thank you, Uncle Silas, for everything." She gave him a hug that made him blush.

Thursday, Jeanette got a cautious go ahead from the doctor to resume normal activities and Friday Brad picked her up for a movie. The story itself wasn't too bad, she decided, but, as she explained to Brad later at the ice cream parlor, "the language was awful and those bed scenes. They didn't need to be in there at all. It's so depressing to see movies like that."

Brad sipped his malt before replying. "Really, Jeanette. You can't live in your secure little fantasy forever. That is the real world. I may not like everything that goes on, but I am strong enough to deal with it."

He took her hand. "You've been sheltered all your life. I want to help you crawl out of your cocoon and fly."

"If that means going against everything I believe in..." Jeanette jammed her straw into the ice cream of her root beer float.

Squeezing her hand, Brad reassured her. "Of course not, but we must live in today's world, not in some idealistic past. Principles are important, loyalty is important, but they must be shaped by reality."

"Jesus never changes," put in Jeanette, troubled at Brad's attitude, but unable to put her feelings into words.

She was relieved when several members of the youth group swung into the door. Seeing her, they waved and crowded around.

"How are you doing? Are you all right?" Jessica hugged her. "Missed you Wednesday night. John, too." She grinned.

"Darilyn said you'll be returning to school on Monday." Josh added. "Hope you didn't get too far behind in your classes. We've missed you at the store." Mischievously he added, "John's been a bear since you've been laid up. You gotta come back so he'll simmer down to something approximating human."

"Darilyn?" Jeanette picked out her friend as the safest topic. She ignored the scowl on Brad's face.

"Yeah, Darilyn." Jessica punched her brother's arm and made him duck. "Your friend came to youth group last night. I think brother here has a crush on her."

Josh covered her mouth with his hand and dragged her to a nearby table. "Come on guys, let Jeanette be. She didn't ask us to join her on her date." Laughing, the group sat down, teasing each other and the waitress as they noisily ordered.

His manner brusque, Brad asked, "Are you finished?"

She wasn't, but Jeanette got to her feet anyway. As they neared the door, Josh called out. "Oh, Jeanette. Paul's Marks are planning a picnic in a couple of weeks. You can tell John." Glancing from her to Brad, he grinned. Jeanette blushed, knowing Josh thought very highly of John.

"John. Always John," Brad muttered as he got into the car beside her.

"Do you want to attend youth group with me?" Jeanette invited. "You're more than welcome." Jeanette bit her lip. Not really sure of his commitment to Christ, she thought it might do him good to attend, but if he did she would miss her time with John.

She wondered both at her sadness and at her relief when he quickly dismissed her idea.

CHAPTER TEN:

The day of the picnic dawned bright and warm. The snow was all but gone, except for patches here and there under the tall park trees. Jeanette preferred the natural setting of Memorial Park to City Park near the campus.

During the week, she'd spent a good deal of time with Brad. He walked to her to and from all her classes and appropriated her lunch periods. Under his care, she felt protected and somewhat overwhelmed.

Never did he let her forget he sought a closer relationship, maybe a permanent one. Yet, something held her back.

Oak, Elm and evergreen trees stood over the sprawling park area like sentinels. Instead of carefully tended gardens, flowers bloomed throughout the park as though scattered by a capricious wind. Dark wood rustic-looking picnic tables graced the park under the protection of the trees. Even the restrooms blended into the scenery.

A stream chortled through the park, splitting it in two with a rustic footbridge completing the idealistic setting. Across the road to the west was a nine-hole golf course while to the north of the park a high fence enclosed a play area of swings, teeter-totters and several merry-go-rounds in different shapes. The delighted screams of children playing drifted over to where the

Paul's Marks youth group gathered together several picnic tables so they could eat together as a group.

Jeanette hailed Darilyn who arrived juggling several dishes. "Oh, John, look. She needs help."

John winked at her when Josh hurried to Darilyn. "I got it," Josh said, taking the heaviest casserole dish from her.

Everyone pitched in to spread the repast on the tables they'd covered with bright table cloths. Taking Jeanette's hand, John pulled her down beside him at the table. As the others found their places, Rev. Connors nodded toward John, "Will you bless this food, John."

John bowed his head, "Lord Jesus. We thank you for this opportunity to get together. I pray you will mold each one of us into your image, committing ourselves to you and you alone. Bless this time of food and fellowship, in your name."

Jeanette squeezed his hand. When he prayed, she was humbled by the depth of his walk. But, as always, the moment she warmed toward John, the teasing began and the moment of closeness passed.

It was almost as though John feared she would get too close. She shook her head; she was being silly. The movement brought a sharp pain to her forehead.

Seeing her grimace, John whispered. "Your head again?"

Jeanette nodded. "It's all right." Though the flesh wound healed from the accident, she still suffered headaches. It wasn't something she advertised, so Darilyn, Josh and the others missed the exchange.

Only John realized that it grew worse as they ate. Afterward, Rev. Connors had a short devotional before the group scattered; some to play touch football, some to talk.

"Let's take a walk," John suggested, helping Jeanette to her feet. He put an arm about her waist, and they sauntered through the park. Arriving at the footbridge, Jeanette walked to the middle and leaned over to watch the catfish splash and dance in the cool clear river. Overhead in the trees, birds trilled and squirrels chattered among the branches.

John joined her. "Feeling better?"

She nodded, wishing the moment could go on forever. It was so peaceful here with John, who fit into the natural setting just as Brad fit the sculptured beauty of City Park with its Olympic style swimming pool.

Mentally she compared the two men; both were tall, though John had several inches on Brad. John had a depth of faith Brad seemed to lack. To be fair, she could not be certain of that since Brad told her when she inquired too deeply, "My faith is a private thing. I'm a good man, I go to church, and I believe in God...in Jesus. That's all that's important. I don't question your personal belief in God, and I will not be interrogated about mine."

His answer left her troubled, but he cut her off whenever she approached the subject until she let it drop all together. She continued to pray for him. It concerned her, because she knew she could not be unequally yoked.

She blushed softly, thinking about Brad's ardent wooing. When she was with Brad, her heart beat faster. When he smiled at her, she melted. But, once she returned from being with Brad, doubts disturbed her. She still heard rumors of him and Tony, though he denied any commitment to her. She wondered about his faith, worried at fitting into his lifestyle.

Even with her talents as designer and seamstress, she doubted she could afford the expense of dressing to please Brad. He refused to discuss the matter, telling her, "Don't worry about that. You'll be fine, Jeanette. You're just what I've been searching for. A lovely young woman willing to let me guide her."

He waved aside her questions and hesitancy with kisses that stole the doubts from her thoughts, until she returned home. Around John, those questions loomed even larger, and she would have liked to discuss the problem with John, but feared he would turn her doubts into one of his jokes.

As much as she liked his sense of humor, sometimes his jokes distanced her from him. She was never quite sure what tack John would take when she was with him. She knew he was concerned about her continuing headaches and blamed himself.

"Dollar for your thoughts."

Jeanette started, her leg hitting a strut of the bridge. "Ow. Umm." She rubbed her leg.

John's eyes were alight with mischief. "I could do that."

Jeanette responded, "Have to catch me first." She took off running, dodging trees and tables. Tackling her, John held her down as she caught her breath. "You're not even winded," she cried with injured pride.

Throwing back his head, John laughed. Staring down at her, he sobered. Leaning down, he touched his lips to hers, softly, reverently, leaving Jeanette staring up at him in wonder. Her emotions whirled in confusion.

The next moment, John's face clouded and almost brusquely he pulled her to her feet. "Forgive me," he muttered. They returned to the others in silence.

Without telling Brad about the kiss, Jeanette tried to get from him some insight into John's behavior. "One minute he is fun, the next his jokes get out of hand. Sometimes I think he likes me, then again..."

Brad pulled her close. "Forget him, Jeanette. He's far too moody for a girl like you. Say you'll marry me, and John will never bother you again."

Yet Jeanette stalled. She enjoyed her time with John, enjoyed long walks in the park with him, which became a regular occurrence for them. Often, they sat on the bench beside the footbridge and watched the fish dance and flash in the sunlight.

Diligently she read her Bible, seeking to find an affirmative answer for Brad. She petitioned, rather badgered, the Heavenly Father for a definite answer. She did want God's will, didn't she? But, what if she didn't like His choice for her? On one hand, she felt a spiritual bond with John, but whenever she thought he was about to tell her he cared, he'd suddenly distance himself. It made no sense to her. In those times, she basked in Brad's open pursuit. On the other hand, Brad often discomfited her with a certain arrogance about his position in society.

As the days passed, Jeanette spent more and more time on her school projects, determined to make the Dean's List. Brad applauded her effort and often picked her up after work so they could study together at the library.

One afternoon when Brad came to pick her up after closing, he found John, Jeanette and the others putting things in order for the next day. This was often a time John pulled some of his more famous pranks. Before Brad could stop him, John crept up on Jeanette. Grabbing the class ring from her finger, he tossed it into the air.

"Catch it," he called, laughing.

Jeanette squealed in alarm as it sailed passed Brad into the hands of a bag boy who tossed it back to John.

Jeanette bit her lip to keep from screaming. "John, don't you realize what Dad sacrificed so I could have that ring?"

Deliberately, John baited Brad. "My ring, my girl," he taunted. Again he tossed it up. The ring arched high into the air and began to descend. As they both reached for it, John collided with Brad who roughly pushed him away.

"Watch where you're going--boy!"

John's face darkened. His hands came up fisted, ready to fight. Thinking both of her ring, and of what her

uncle would say if John and Brad fought in the store,
Jeanette stepped between them "My ring?"

Immediately, everyone set about searching for one
small ring in the midst of aisles and aisles of food stuffs,
boxes and supplies. No one discovered the ring.

Finally, John shrugged. "Sorry, Jeanette, guess it's
gone for good." Pivoting on his heels, he left her
standing in shock at his callousness.

Angry tears stung her eyes. Without a word, Brad led
her out to his car. Taking her to a private place, Brad
parked the car and took Jeanette into his arms as she
wept out her anger and sense of betrayal.

"How could John be so casual about my ring? It was
my cl…class ring. He doesn't even have one." It
occurred to her that maybe John had not been able to
afford one, but she was too distraught to be charitable.

"I warned you about him, my dear." Brad said,
adding, "Forget that paltry ring. Marry me, and I
promise you'll have everything your little heart desires. I
know how to treat my lady."

Hurt and angry over John's indifference, Jeanette
sighed. "Maybe you're right, Brad, right about
everything." Maybe Brad was God's plan for her.

Why not accept Brad's offer, she thought. Obviously
John didn't care about her feelings. This last was just
one of the many things he had done to distance her, and,
unlike Brad, he'd never given her hope that he wanted
more from her than friendship.

Lifting her chin, she told him firmly. "Yes, Brad, I
will marry you."

Yet, the kiss he brushed against her lips left her feeling vaguely cheated.

A large engagement ring soon replaced the lost class ring, and Jeanette basked in the envy and well-wishes of her friends. That both Brad's parents and her aunt and uncle seemed less than enthusiastic, she shrugged off. She was sorry, too, to hurt her uncle and aunt when she, at Brad's insistence, switched to Brad's church. After all, she'd be joining it once they married.

Aunt Evelyn simply told her, "Pray about it, dear."

She smiled at their concern. "I'll do that."

Unfortunately, Jeanette found herself drawn, often reluctantly, into the swirl of Brad's social activities. That, along with her press to finish the year at the top of her class, left her exhausted and with little time for either reflection--or prayer.

What hurt even more was the tension between her and John. He never mentioned the ring again, neither did she, but that and her engagement hung between them like an open wound.

By the time school dismissed for the summer, Jeanette found herself relieved to go home and away from McFadden. Next fall would be time enough to mend her fences with John.

CHAPTER ELEVEN:

The late afternoon sun glinted off the windows of the large old fashion farm house that glistened with its fresh coat of paint as Jeanette rounded the bend in Sandie's car. The yard appeared newly mown and the hedges had been trimmed and shaped.

"The man your dad hired has made quite an improvement in the place." Sandie squinted in the glare of the afternoon sun. "And, of course, your dad has gotten so much better."

"I can't wait to see them. It seems like ages since I've been home." Rolling down the window, she breathed in deeply. "So tell me about this man, Dad hired. What's he like?"

Sandie ran a hand through her short red hair. "Actually, he's real nice. Used to farm himself until he lost his wife." Jeanette listened to her friend, glad Sandie insisted on coming to get her. It had been nice to catch up with each other's lives on the long drive home.

She smiled. Most of the time Sandie talked about the wedding, and Jeff, then the wedding some more.

Sandie inquired, her expression held a question. "You do have your dress done?"

"Of course, I do. I did it as a project. I wrote you about it, remember. Got an A in the class."

Sandie threw up a hand. "I never thought I was a scatterbrain until I realized how close the wedding really is. Jeanette within a month, I'll be Mrs. Jeff Swanson. I can't believe it." She shook her head. "Here I'm going on and on, when I want to hear all about your Brad Marsden.

"How did you meet him? What's he like? Is he handsome?"

Laughing, Jeanette regaled her with the 'wonderful' Brad. If Sandie heard an undertone of uncertainty, she kept silent.

Though Jeanette's parents encouraged her to stay for supper, Sandie pleaded another engagement. "With that young man of yours, no doubt," Jeanette's dad teased.

It was good to hear his laughter again. Jeanette recalled how he used to throw her up and catch her as a child and even get down on the floor to play with her. He had a keen sense of humor, reminding her sharply of John. It had been her father's sense of humor she missed most of all after the accident. Yet John's teasing hurt as well as made her laugh.

Thinking of John reminded her also of the hurt between them. With a shake of her head, she determined to banish him from her mind, for the summer at least.

Her mother caught her grimace. "Does your head hurt? Evelyn said you still had some pretty nasty headaches. What did the doctor say about it?"

Jeanette rubbed her forehead in a gesture that had become characteristic since the accident. "He thinks they'll disappear with time."

At the supper table, she met Troy Hanson, the thin, wiry handyman who had become part of the family during the last semester. Jeanette found him a quiet man and appreciated his sensitivity in excusing himself after supper, leaving her alone with her parents.

"Well," her father asked, settling into his worn green recliner. "I'd like to know about this Brad you've gotten yourself engaged to."

Jeanette heard the mild reproof and bit her lips. "He's real nice, Dad. His family owns Marsden refinery."

"I'm not interested in his background or his wealth. I want to know about the young man who asked for your hand without even having the courtesy to talk it over with us." His glance took in Jeanette's mother, sitting in an upholstered rocker opposite. "He could have at least telephoned to introduce himself."

Sitting on the couch worn low from years of use, and abuse, she thought wryly, recalling the times she had been scolded for jumping on it, Jeanette sighed. "Uncle Silas and Aunt Evelyn know him and his family."

"Then he talked to them."

"We...ll no, but we told them together. At the time, I was very upset over something that happened at the store."

"Will we meet him this summer, Jean?" her mother asked, using the nick name Jeanette had never liked.

"No. He's going to Europe with his parents this summer and won't return until just before classes begin."

Jeanette wasn't sure how she survived her parents' grilling, however good intentioned, but if her answers did not entirely satisfy them, they left it with, "We're here if you ever want to talk. We'll be praying for both you and Brad."

"Sandie says her father will take me on at the store in Colby for the summer." Jeanette told her folks. "So I'll at least be able to earn something during my time at home. Unless, you need my help here."

"No, Troy is a God send. I don't know why I was so stubborn about hiring someone. It wasn't until Silas pointed out what I was doing to you, and offered to help out with your tuition..." his words trailed off in embarrassment.

Jeanette's head snapped up. "I had no idea. But, Dad, I'm glad I stayed home and went to Colby Community College. I don't think I was ready to leave home right out of high school."

Her mother's smile warmed her heart, and they moved on to more general topics. Later, as Jeanette prepared for bed in her spacious, if sparsely, furnished room at the top of the stairs, she reflected on the evening. She enjoyed the time with her folks, and hoped there would be many more leisurely evenings with them.

And there were. Many an evening, she sat with her mother and father out on the lawn enjoying the colorful sunset and talking. By this time, Jeanette, too, accepted Troy, and did not mind when he sometimes joined them.

Of course more often, Troy and her father were busy in the fields. She also found her days filled. Four days a

week she worked 8:45 am. to 5:30 pm. for Sandie's
father. With a semester behind her in her Uncle's store,
she felt confident in her new position. Silas asked her to
stay on over the summer, but understood her desire to be
home. Besides, Jeanette didn't want her aunt and uncle
to worry about her when they were visiting their
daughter Janice and family in Texas where her husband
pastored a church.

After work, she often stayed in town with Sandie,
going over and over each detail of the wedding plans. As
the wedding approached, Sandie grew more and more
nervous.

"Sometimes I wish we could just elope. It would be
so much easier," she complained. "I just know
something is going to go wrong."

"Not when you have the right man," Jeanette
responded teasingly, but the sentiment stuck in her
throat.

As the days wore on, her doubts about her decision
to marry Brad also grew. There were times she ached to
share her hesitancy with Sandie, but couldn't bear to add
to her problems. She feared talking to her folks as well,
especially after their latest ordeal over Cynthia.

Her sister, as usual, dropped in unannounced, excited
about her latest deal; a part in a movie. "I'm really and
truly going to be an actress," she cried.

Her eyes narrowed as she saw Troy standing in the
doorway, waiting quietly to speak with her father. She
took in his wind-blown dark hair, his lean body, and
ready smile.

Cynthia gave him the once-over. "Who are you?".

Standing, her father made the introductions. "Cynthia Harvey, Troy Hanson. Troy, our daughter Cynthia."

Jeanette did not like the hungry look in Cynthia's eyes. She knew the look and worried about Troy. She was right to worry. None of them realized what Cynthia was about until Troy asked her father for her hand. Her father was stunned, what could he say to Troy about his daughter?

His confrontation with Cynthia made the rafters shake. Cynthia merely laughed at Troy's naiveté. The next morning she left without a word. Troy hid his hurt under an uncertain smile that tore at Jeanette's heart. Overhearing her parents talking one night, she was thankful she had not shared her doubts with them.

"I am ashamed that Cynthia is my daughter," her father sighed. "The girl has no sense of decency, and no idea of what commitment is all about. How dare she lead Troy into believing she would marry him?" He groaned, and Jeanette pictured him putting his head in his hands.

Her mother soothed him. "It's not your fault. Cynthia made her choices. But we can still pray for her. God does keep His promises, and He did promise." She quoted softly, "'Train up a child in the way he should go: and when he is old, he will not depart from it.' We must stand on that promise." She continued brokenly, "Besides, right now, we could not have blessed this marriage anyway, Cynthia is not a believer. She seems totally incapable of keeping commitments."

Jeanette closed her eyes. She'd made a commitment to Brad, there was no going back now--was there? At times, she wondered not only about the depth of Brad's faith, but about the depth of her own love for Brad. Why was it she felt secure in their love only when she was with him?

His letters helped allay some of her fears. They were full of brochures and pictures and descriptions of all the places he had visited, along with flowing words that made her blush.

"I am already planning our honeymoon, darling. We're going on the most romantic European vacation ever." Jeanette bit her lip, irritated that Brad was not even considering her wishes in his plans for them. Still, a European vacation.

"You're kidding." Sandie smiled dreamily, "That's great for you, but I'm glad Jeff and I planned ours together."

Sandie's wedding went off with only minor disasters, and none of them bothered the bride who swept through the afternoon in a daze. Before the ceremony she did comment on how lovely her maid of honor looked in her formal gown of rich lace over dusty pink. As they stood at the altar, Jeanette's mind turned to John and she wondered if the hurt between them bothered him as much as it bothered her.

"Oh, bother! Why was she thinking of John now?" Deliberately Jeanette turned her thoughts toward Brad.

CHAPTER TWELVE:

Though the summer had been a pleasant interlude, Jeanette found herself more than ready to return to school. After Sandie left on her honeymoon, the summer seemed to drag, despite outings with other high school friends to the lake, to the country fair and to church.

Darilyn's visit just before school began in September provided a welcome diversion. She had been delighted with the big open farm, the lake and the country church. The girls talked late into the night, and often Jeanette arrived at work yawning.

Darilyn timed her visit so she could drive Jeanette back to McFadden. She patted her ancient Chevy. "It isn't much to look at, but my oldest brother is a mechanic, and he keeps it running."

"I wish I had a car," Jeanette said, as they headed down highway 70 East. "At least, I wouldn't have to beg rides."

Darilyn laughed. "But I loved an excuse to come now. And we'll have just that much more time to talk."

"About Joshua?" Jeanette's eyes danced, and it was her friend who blushed. "You must get a letter from him every other day."

"He is nice, but we're just friends--at this stage," she cautioned. "I want to be very sure he's the right one before I make any commitments."

Jeanette pursed her lips. "How do you know if someone is the right one? I don't mean the movie stuff where two people gaze at each other across a room and the next minute they're in bed together."

Darilyn glanced at her in surprise. Seeing the serious expression on Jeanette's face, Darilyn said thoughtfully, "Of course, we both know that's something very different from the love God offers us. His love is sacrificial and giving. I guess if we love someone, we will want what is best for that person. Ephesians 6 says we are to submit to our husbands and respect them. That would be one key, I guess. If I didn't feel I could trust someone with my life or respect them and their decisions... Why? Are you having second thoughts?"

Flipping back her long braid, Jeanette stared out over the rolling prairies all green and golden with corn and wheat. "Not when I'm with Brad."

"You have doubts?" Darilyn asked. "You do love him, don't you?"

Jeanette forced a laugh. "Of course I do." But the doubt lingered.

"If you're not sure..."

"I've made a promise, Dari, I will keep my promise." She turned to Darilyn. "All summer long, I've been doing a study on faithfulness. God is faithful to us and expects us to be faithful in our commitments as well." Her lips tightened as she thought of her sister, and

Troy's quiet pain. "It may be the fashionable thing to break promises these days, but I've seen the hurt of broken promises."

"So have I," Darilyn commented. "Nevertheless, it's important to be sure, Jeanette. Make certain Brad is God's best for you."

Jeanette's heart sank. She was not sure, not sure at all, but she'd made a commitment--and she would keep it. Verses she memorized during her summer search filled her mind: "for the Lord preserveth the faithful*; He that is faithful in that which is least is faithful also in much*."

Darilyn interrupted her thoughts, "At least, you have time to decide. Have you even set a wedding date yet?"

Shaking her head, Jeanette said, "That's something we have yet to decide and went on to tell Darilyn about Brad's plans for their honeymoon."

Her parents sent her off with prayers and hugs, and Jeanette's aunt and uncle welcomed her the same way, making her feel both wanted and loved. It was a good feeling that lasted until she saw Brad.

Jeanette spent part of her summer carefully sewing several new outfits to add to her wardrobe for the school year. She hoped Brad would approve her chic new look.

Her heart fluttered as she waited for him to pick her up. She checked her hair in the mirror hoping he would like the new way she wore her hair, up, with tendrils curling about her oval face. Critically, she surveyed her new lavender silk-look, three piece suit and smoothed the skirt that swirled softly over her hips to her knees. The top (which she had embroidered herself), peeked out from the shawl collar of the over the hip jacket.

Coming into the room, Evelyn nodded her approval. "It's lovely, my dear. Why you couldn't find anything better in that fancy boutique downtown."

Jeanette smiled. "Thank you. I wouldn't even have attempted such a project, especially not the jacket, before last semester."

Her aunt's approval gave her confidence to face Brad whose eyes lit up with appreciation. "Perfect." Taking her arm, he led her to the car.

Getting in on the other side, he studied her lovely profile. Reaching over, he stroked her cheek. "I missed you," he said softly.

Jeanette's heart sang. Suddenly, all her doubts seemed foolish and far away. "Oh, Brad, I missed you, too. I hope we never have to spend so much time apart again."

Her declaration pleased him immensely.

Once more they dined in the Victorian House in Hutchinson. This time the manager acknowledged her presence with a stiff smile. "Congratulations, Mr. Marsden."

Jeanette blushed. "They knew we were engaged," she whispered after they were seated and Brad had ordered for them.

True he did not ask her preference, but it was a minor irritation in the excitement of being near him again. She melted under his smile.

"Of course they know, Darling. It is their business to know." He eyed her outfit. "I'm glad you wore such a becoming outfit. Don't tell me you made it."

"All right, I won't tell you, but I did. I'm glad you approve." Jeanette could not stop the silly smile that kept spreading across her face.

"You got my letters?"

"Yes," she sighed, "you sounded like you had a terrific time."

Reaching for her hand, Brad made Jeanette blush as he placed light kisses on her palm. "But it will be much more enjoyable when we see Europe together."

On the way home, Brad cleared his throat. "About our wedding."

Jeanette tensed. "Yes."

He flashed her an apologetic smile. "We haven't discussed a wedding date."

"Oh," Jeanette choked out a laugh, earning her a quizzical and slightly disapproving glance. "Oh Brad, I thought you were going to cry off."

"Cry off, you mean call off the wedding." He squeezed her hand. "No chance of that."

Jeanette offered, "A Christmas wedding might be nice."

Brad hesitated. "I don't think so, Jeanette. This Christmas we would not be out of school yet, and I'm not about to wait until the next Christmas." He smiled at her.

"I discussed the date with mother. A May wedding would fit into her plans very nicely. There are so many

plans to make. Besides, you do understand, I couldn't possibly get married until after I graduate."

"You talked our wedding over with your mother, before you talked to me?" Jeanette was hard put to disguise her distress. "Wait a minute. What plans?"

"Why the church, caterers, hall for the reception..."

While her headaches came less frequently, she rubbed her forehead, feeling one coming on. "Church here? I plan to be married at home."

Brad's smile failed to soothe her. "I know you did, Darling, but you have to be realistic. Do you really think your home church is large enough for all the people we must invite? We must think of who we are. Like it or not, Darling, you are marrying the Marsden heir, and my folks want to do this up right."

"What about my parents?"

Brad's lips tightened. "I would think, they would be thankful not to have the burden of the wedding on them. Tell me, Jeanette. Can they really afford the kind of wedding my folks expect?"

Gulping back her tears, Jeanette shook her head. From the time she was small, she had dreamed of walking down the aisle of their little country church on her father's arm. But Brad was right, as usual.

He smiled his approval at her submission. "Our Senator, maybe even the Governor will attend. What do you think of that?"

Jeanette couldn't bring herself to cry as she sadly put away the dreams for a small simple wedding of family and close friends. "It's fine, I guess."

She made one more attempt. "Couldn't we have just a small wedding? We could have it here in McFadden in my aunt and uncle's church."

"My mother would faint with shock. No, we must humor her, Darling." Stopping the car in her driveway, he pulled her into his arms. His kisses somehow failed to soothe the pain in her heart, and she pulled away.

It wasn't to be her only shock.

The next morning, she got her class schedule. It felt good to already know her way around the campus; and good to be a senior. More than once she assisted a lost, panicky freshman to find her way around what had been a maze to her so recently. She and Darilyn laughed about her own frustration when she first arrived.

At lunch, she told Darilyn about the wedding.

"So you are going through with it?"

"Why of course, that was never in doubt. Brad was very nice about it. He's correct one thing; it would be much easier financially if my parents don't have to pay for the wedding. I just hope they won't be insulted." She sighed. "I want you as one of my bridesmaids. Sandie has to be my maid of honor, though, as I was for her."

"Of course. I'll be thrilled to stand up for you." She giggled. "Now, if you could talk Brad into asking Josh to stand up for him."

Jeanette rolled her eyes. "Sure. Come on, eat up or we'll be late for class."

Though Jeanette protested, her uncle again made her get used to her class routine before allowing her to work. The first day she entered the store again, her heart pounded for she had considered and set aside more than one actual written apology to John.

She need not have worried because he was not in the store. She assumed he'd been sent to another store, but by the end of the week, Jeanette was seriously concerned.

Sunday over Brad's protests, she attended services with her aunt and uncle. "Aunt Evelyn and Uncle Silas would like me to continue going to their church until we're married. It's the least I can do for them for being so kind to me. Why don't you go with me?"

Brad shook his head. "I don't think so." Leaning over he kissed her. "I don't like it, but I am glad to see your concern for your uncle." He grinned, "Never hurts to keep up the business contacts."

Tracing her frowning lips, he said, "I'm teasing." But Jeanette again felt a nagging doubt. Business and status did seem to occupy a high priority for him.

"What about Paul's Marks on Wednesday, will you go?"

"I don't think so," he told her, and she left it at that.

Rev. Connors sermon brought a measure of peace to her troubled heart, and she soaked up the worshipful atmosphere. Afterward, unobtrusively she tried to spot John. Instead, she saw only his mother with another woman of about the same age, but obviously in much better health.

Later that afternoon, she questioned her uncle. "Uncle Silas. I didn't see John in church today. In fact, I haven't seen him at the store either. Is he all right?"

Her uncle eyes darkened. "John is gone, Jeanette."

"Gone," she echoed, fear clawing at her throat.

"He joined the Marines." He told her, "He left a few days before you returned."

Anger flared. "What about his mother?"

"He was able to persuade her widowed aunt to come live with her."

"Where did he go? Will he been home again soon? Jeanette asked, hoping there would still be an opportunity to make things right.

"I'm sorry, Jeanette, but no. John went to MEPS in Kansas City."

"What?"

"Oh, yes," Silas said, "you don't understand. You know both our Randy and Jim joined the marines so it is as they say 'old hat' to me. MEPS is the Military Entrance Processing Station. He went on to the recruit depo in San Diego. He'll be there for about 12 weeks with no leave."

"Then he can come home?"

Silas considered her thoughtfully. Jeanette bit her lip praying he wouldn't question her reasons and sighed with relief when he merely said, "From there he goes for schooling. Then he'll be stationed at Camp Pendleton in California."

"I see, but he could come home for a visit."

"Yes, he does get 30 days paid leave a year."

"How long?"

"Four years."

"Four years! But, Uncle Silas, why? Why did he suddenly join the marines?" She sobered. "Will he be sent overseas?"

Her Uncle nodded slowly, and Jeanette sensed he knew why John enlisted, but felt unable to break the young man's confidence.

Jeanette excused herself. In her room, she berated herself for not making things right with John before she left for the summer. Now it was too late. Inside, she felt a void, a void not entirely erased by Brad's attentiveness.

*Psalm 31:23 *Luke 16:10

CHAPTER THIRTEEN:

Brad was attentive. One weekend, they attended the McPherson Scottish and Heritage Festival at Lakeside Park in McPherson, featuring music, food, heritage displays and dances, and proudly highlighted the town's own bagpipe band, Jeanette learned, originated with the production of "Brigadoon".

"Scottish bagpipes in a town with a decided Swedish heritage?" Jeanette smiled.

"Of course, Darling. Why not? The Scottish have a proud heritage. My great grandmother came from Scotland."

"I had no idea. So how did she end up in Kansas?"

"It's a long story." Brad told her, steering her to toward the tables and booths with different heritage crafts where he purchased a carefully worked tartan shawl he placed about her shoulders.

Later that afternoon, they attended the Old Fashioned Harvest Festival featuring pioneer arts, crafts, and activities at the McPherson Museum.

Jeanette gulped at the large check Brad wrote out to the museum. "Good public relations," he told her with a grin.

Despite his rather mercenary gift, Jeanette really enjoyed the afternoon. Certainly, she enjoyed those

private times with Brad much more than the receptions and meetings and other events he felt obligated to attend.

For the reception Brad's mother orchestrated to formally announce the engagement, Jeanette again wore the lavender suit, though Brad encouraged her to buy something new. "Mother will help you pick it out."

Jeanette sucked in a quick breath. "You don't trust my judgment in clothes?"

Brad tugged a stray lock and tucked it behind her ear. "Of course, Darling, but there will be some very important people there. If it's a matter of money, I'll...."

"You will nothing. I will not have you paying for my clothes before we're married, Brad Marsden. And if you are so ashamed of my taste...."

His kiss smothered her indignation. "I apologize. But you will wear your hair up." He studied her thoughtfully. "Ever think of cutting your hair? I think you'd look great with it around your face."

"You really think so?"

"I do. It would give Mother pleasure to do this for you." When she hesitated, Brad coaxed. "It would give you an opportunity to get better acquainted."

Jeanette acquiesced. She wasn't sure which she feared most, a whole new look or being alone with Brad's mother. For all her kindness, Jeanette sensed Brad's mother was disappointed her son had chosen a nobody for his wife.

Nonetheless, Mrs. Marsden did her best with Jeanette, taking her to Wichita for a complete facial and makeover. For some time, Mrs. Marsden and the hairdresser discussed length and style. Intimidated, Jeanette bit her lip and kept her concerns to herself.

Feeling the scissors clipping away the long hair, Jeanette closed her eyes. "Please Lord, let it be all right." She couldn't help recalling John's tender touch on her hair the night they'd eaten pizza together.

The pleased expression on Mrs. Marsden's face gave Jeanette the confidence to check the mirror herself. She was astounded at the change the hair cut, perm and makeup made in her appearance. For a moment, she wondered who the sophisticated young woman was. Brad was equally pleased.

The night of the reception, Mrs. Marsden appeared relieved at Jeanette's choice of outfit. "Why it is lovely? Brad said you made all your own clothes."

Resentment burned momentarily, just what had Brad said about her? "Most of them anyway." she responded sweetly.

Tony, came up then, glass in hand. Her sweeping gaze missed nothing. "You made that, I suppose."

"Actually I did."

Tony surveyed her again. "Maybe, I'll have to have you whip something up for me."

Jeanette flushed at the implication she was no better than a hired seamstress. Noticing the amber liquid in Tony's glass, she cast a questioning glance toward Brad who shrugged.

She had little time to question him further, because Mrs. Marsden took charge of her, taking her around the room to introduce her. Names and faces blurred. Someone stuck a glass in her hand, but after a sniff at the contents, Jeanette managed to pass it off to one of the waiters who continually circulated among the guests with drinks and sandwiches and other foods she could not identify.

When Brad moved on to speak to some of his friends, Jeanette felt very out of place and alone. Awkwardly, she sipped the pop she had finally managed to procure. Glancing up, she found Tony watching her with a certain disdain.

"How did you do it?" she asked.

"Do?" Jeanette wished Brad would come to her side.

"How did you manage to get Brad to ask you to marry him? None of the others managed that." Her slightly unfocused gaze discomfited Jeanette. Obviously, Tony had been drinking. "I underestimated you." She raised her glass in salute. "To the bride to be." she called loudly, starting the cry as others raised their glasses to her.

Jeanette was never so glad to leave a place in her life. Trembling with anger and humiliation, Jeanette woodenly sat in the car as Brad drove her home.

"I'm sorry about Tony."

Jeanette turned on him. "Tony was the least of it. Brad, you know how I feel about alcoholic beverages. Why didn't you tell me?"

"It didn't occur to me. Be realistic, Jeanette. I think your stand is admirable. I feel the same way."

She accused, "You had a drink in your hand all evening."

"Social reasons only. Did you ever see me drink it?"

"I suppose that's merely for good public relations." Sarcasm bit her words.

"Social relations, anyway."

Jeanette's lips tightened. "I want you to know right now, Brad Marsden; I will not have alcoholic beverages served in my house."

"Our house, Darling. I'm sorry, all right. But its over."

"I'm not kidding, Brad. If it happens again, I will walk out."

Brad frowned. "If it means that much to you. I'm sure mother can concoct some punch substitute."

Tears stung Jeanette's eyes. "Brad, I'm not trying to be difficult."

His arm pulled her close; his mouth stopped her words. "I know Darling. Just be patient with mother. She has her own way of doing things. After we're married, we can do things any way we want."

Their next difference came even more unexpectedly and caused Jeanette more hurt. After a light snow, Indian summer came to warm the fall air. Overhead, leaves turned to red and gold and sifted down on the students as they hurried to their classes. Flocks of birds lighted on the tree branches, chirping as though making plans for their flight north.

Darilyn hurried beside Josh who carried her bookbag. Behind them, Brad walked beside Jeanette.

Finishing their last class of the morning, they headed toward the cafeteria.

Sitting down with her roast beef plate and milk, Jeanette turned to Brad. "Guess what I chose to make for my formal gown."

Fastidiously, Brad opened and carefully poured his pop into a glass. "I have no idea."

"My wedding dress." Her excitement bubbled over. "I get to design it and chose the material. I have the lace all picked out..."

Brad's silence finally penetrated. "What's wrong, Brad?" she faltered. "Don't you like the idea? Even your mother agrees I have talent."

"I'm sure it would do fine for your home church, but ...." He patted her hand in a condescending manner he had adopted. "I would hate to see you embarrassed in front of the guests. I wouldn't want...."

Jeanette flushed angrily, "to be ashamed of your bride's wedding gown."

Brad cleared his throat. "Maybe if you'd show your designs to mother or...or Tony."

He quickly backed down. "All right. Tony is a bad idea, even if she does have good taste in clothes."

"And I haven't. If you insist, I will show them to your mother." She was gratified with the older woman's frank praise at her talents.

"Jeanette, your design is lovely and quite smart. You show real talent. Maybe it is something we can encourage once you're married. A boutique maybe of your own designs."

The idea excited Jeanette, but Brad was less than enthusiastic. "Mother sometimes has big dreams, Jeanette, but it's a long way from designing a few clothes for yourself to being able to turn a profit from doing the same thing on a regular basis for others. Besides," he said, smiling that smile that usually made her weak, "I'd like my wife available."

Jeanette blushed at his implication and pulled away. No matter what she did, it never quite met with Brad's approval.

At night, Jeanette read her Bible, but the words seemed cold and dead, and her prayers fruitless. In church, she found a measure of peace, but always there was an underlying discontent. Brad's church, which she finally consented to attend once a month, left her feeling even more alienated and alone. There was a growing void in her life, a void having nothing to do with John whom she continued to miss.

She had one consolation. In exchange for her attendance at Brad's church, he agreed to attend Paul's Marks with her. He was even more enthusiastic when he got to pick her up after work and take her out for supper beforehand. It was the only date she allowed herself during the week because of her school work. At times, she cooked supper for them all, finding Brad as enthusiastic about her pecan pie as her uncle.

She wished she could talk to someone about the frustration and anger and hurt building up inside her. God seemed so far away. She didn't want to hurt her aunt and uncle or through them, alert her parents to her

growing discontent about her relationship with Brad.
Brad, too, sometimes seemed more sober of late.

As for Darilyn, she was completely caught up with
Josh. She'd never been all that close to Jessica. She
debated calling Sandie, but her friend was settling in to
her new life.

"God help me," she cried into her pillow. She missed
the close communion she once had with her Lord. It was
gone, and Jeanette did not know what to do to restore it.

Did all brides to be go through this? No, it had been
very different for Sandie.

"You have the right man." The jest played over and
over in her mind, only it wasn't funny any more.

There had to be another answer.

The second week in October, Brad got her uncle to
give her Saturday off. His eyes brimming with his
secret, he told her to dress casually. Jeanette's doubt and
confusion faded under the light of his attentiveness. She
should be, was, grateful for Brad.

"Where are we going?" she asked, as he urged the
car onto the highway.

"We celebrated my heritage," he told her, "now we
celebrate yours."

For the first time in weeks, Jeanette relaxed,
enjoying being with Brad as he amused her with bits of
gossip and incidents from the refinery.

It wasn't until they drew close to Lindsborg that he
grinned. "The Svensk Hyllningsfest."

Her sudden intake of breath, he took as pleased
surprise. Parking the car, he led her about town. Pasting

a smile on her face, Jeanette watched the parade of dancers and bands and floats. She marveled at all the colorful authentic costumes. She ate authentic Swedish cookies and cakes, but tasted nothing.

As Brad escorted her through the quaint shops lining the street, her anger turned on John. He had promised to take her to this fest, and he had broken his promise. Deliberately, she tried to force her thoughts from that special day with John and its near disaster aftermath when he saved her life.

Brad watched as she rubbed her forehead more and more frequently. "Headache?"

Biting her lip against the pain, Jeanette nodded. "I'm sorry, Brad, but could you take me home."

He nodded. With gentleness, he assisted her into the car and headed back toward McFadden. "Is there something I can do?"

Guiltily, Jeanette glanced out the window. It wasn't Brad's fault she hadn't had a good time. Would Lindsborg always remind her of John?

When she returned home her aunt met her with the news. "John's mother was taken to the hospital this afternoon."

CHAPTER FOURTEEN

"Oh, no. What happened? Is she all right?" Jeanette forgot her headache in her concern. "How did you find out?"

"Her sister called the prayer chain. I just got word a few minutes ago." She held out her hand. "Would you pray with me?"

"Of course, I will," she hastened to say, adding with a self-deprecating laugh, "but my own prayers haven't seemed too effective these days."

Jeanette missed her aunt's reflective glance as she sat down beside her aunt on the couch. Her aunt bowed her head. "Dear Lord, we lift up Catherine Amory to you. Jesus, you know what the problem is far more than we, and you are the creator and healer and savior of us all. Please touch our sister Catherine and make her whole again. In the name of Jesus." She waited quietly for Jeanette who hesitated, realizing just how long it had been since she had prayed with someone else.

Her face burned, and she was glad her aunt's head remained bowed. "Lord, Jesus," she stuttered. Clearing her throat she began again. "Lord, I know you love Mrs. Amory. Please take care of her. And help them be able to get the news to John."

"Thank you Lord," finished her aunt. After squeezing Jeanette's hand, she released it, and looked up with a smile.

"Jeanette, maybe you could tell me what's on your heart."

Jeanette blushed and stared down at the carpet. Her words rushed out, "Oh, Aunt Evelyn, sometimes I am so mixed up about things."

"What things, dear?" The kind expression on her aunt's face encouraged her.

"I love Brad, and I am promised to marry him, but...but sometimes I have doubts about us. Did you ever wonder if Uncle Silas was really the one for you?"

Her aunt chuckled softly. "I'll say I did. I'm afraid our courtship was a rather stormy on again off again affair. Believe it or not, your Uncle can be a very stubborn man at times. I always heard about stubborn Swedes, but I think the Roberts and the Swansons (my family, you know) could win prizes."

Jeanette nodded her understanding. "Sounds like Mom. She says Dad is as stubborn as the day is long and that both Cynthia and I take after him."

"Once you make up your mind, it's not easily changed is it?"

Thinking of Cynthia's rebellion, Jeanette shook her head. "If that's true, why do I have doubts?"

Aunt Evelyn measured her words carefully. "Doubts can be Satan's way of breaking down your resistance, but..." she raised a hand in emphasis, "but it can be God's Holy Spirit trying to speak to you."

Confusion crossed Jeanette's face. "How do I know God's will for me?"

"Ah," her aunt voiced her approval, "you're asking the right questions. There are five simple steps to knowing God's will, Jeanette."

Jeanette waited expectantly. Finally, an easy way for her to erase her inner conflicts.

"Prayer is your key. Have you prayed about the problem until you have the assurance of God's peace and the leading of His Holy Spirit through specific Bible passages?" Jeanette swallowed, but did not interrupt her aunt.

"Have you talked over the situation with Godly men or women who can advise you wisely? And, have you taken into consideration all the pros and cons of the decision?"

Shifting, Jeanette hated to admit she hadn't much done any of those things in making her decision to marry Brad. She was hurting and, at the time, he seemed to be the answer to her problem.

Her aunt continued, "All of the others make little difference if your heart isn't ready to receive God's will. Obedience isn't something you do if and when you feel like it. Obedience is willingness to do what God wants you to do before you know what that is. It willingness to obey even when doing so is difficult."

She left Jeanette with much to contemplate. But far from erasing the conflict, the advice brought out the emptiness inside. "Lord," she cried, "please help me know what to do. I want to be faithful. I don't want to fail You, or my folks, or Brad."

While her conflict did not go away, Jeanette made one promise to herself. She would not again neglect her time in God's Word as she had been doing because of her busy schedule. Besides, the Roberts, she thought proudly, keep their promises.

Sunday at church, Rev. Connors announced that John's mother had developed a respiratory infection and would be in the hospital for a week at least. Maybe more, depending on how her weaken system responded to treatment.

Later, Uncle Silas gave her the news, "John is getting a few days hardship leave."

Flushing with a confusion of excitement and fear, Jeanette hurried to her room, hoping her uncle hadn't seen the leap of joy in her eyes at the news.

But she never got a chance to see him. Between his vigil at his mother's bedside and her quick response to treatment, he had already left before Jeanette could figure out a way to approach him. The night she heard the news, she cried herself to sleep. She couldn't let the rift weigh on her any longer, and she knew what she had to do.

A few days later, she had the opportunity to visit John's mother when her aunt asked her to bring Catherine a casserole. Shyly, she asked the woman for John's address. She didn't know if he still had a cell and didn't feel comfortable calling anyway.

That evening, she sat down and wrote John a letter of apology for her part in their misunderstanding. With a sigh, she mailed it before going to classes. Her heart felt just a bit lighter. Singing slightly off key, she swung her bike onto the campus drive.

Stepping off the curb, Brad grabbed her handlebars. "Hey, you're in a good mood today. Here, let me lock up your bike and walk to you to class." He fitted action to words. Taking her bookbag, he flung it over his left shoulder with his own bookbag. His other arm pulled her close. "How's my girl today?" His lips touched hers.

Laughing, she kissed him back. Brad was a handsome, caring man, and she deeply cared for him. "Well, Brad Marsden. Have you decided whether or not you can come home and meet my parents over Thanksgiving? You did say your family made plans w-a-y in advance."

For a moment, he held her closer and her heartbeat quickened. She loved this man with the devastating smile, she did.

"Yes, though we did have plans, both my parents and I feel it is my obligation to meet your folks so they can learn," he mocked himself, "what a wonderful man their daughter is marrying."

They both laughed. "Will you go with me to Paul's Marks again this week."

His smile dimmed and he grimaced. "Do I have to?" he whined.

She grinned, liking his new ability to tease once in a while. It had been missing in their relationship. "You do." She insisted, joy bubbling up inside at his desire to please her in this. Lately, he appeared to almost enjoy the camaraderie of the others, and almost overwhelmed at their easy acceptance of him.

Later, she teased him as he guided his powerful sports car west on the highway. "You're as bad as Josh with your tricks. Why the things he and John used to pull." She stopped at the quizzical look on Brad's face at the mention of John.

Brad asked,. "Have you heard anything about him since he left?"

Jeanette prayed her cheeks would not give her away. She never told Brad about her letter. Not that it mattered, since John hadn't answered it anyway. The thought of his anger festered, but she tried not to think about it.

"From what I understand, his basic training is almost over so he'll soon be transferred to Camp Pendleton. His mother said he's trying to get a job as an administrative clerk. He wants to go on to college." She gulped. "Of course, he may be sent overseas instead."

"Ah, college. I suppose that's why he signed up. I've never liked him much, but I do have to give him credit for trying to get ahead. At least, it's more than his father ever did.

"His father, what about his father?"

Brad shook his head. "You didn't know that John's father up and left his family when he was still in elementary school?"

Jeanette's heart broke for the young John. "How awful."

Brad took in Jeanette's expressive face. "It didn't give John the most stable background."

"Brad," she asked quietly, "is that one of the reasons you tried to steer me away from him?"

He nodded. "That and the fact I was jealous of the time you spent with him. You belonged to me."

"No, Brad, I belong to the Lord." she said firmly, more secure in her relationship to the Lord. Her daily time in His Word had given her that at least, even though her search for answers continued to be frustrating, and her walk was still tenuous.

Brad sobered and remained silent for so long, Jeanette asked, "Is something wrong?"

"I have a confession, Jeanette." His hands on the wheel tightened. "I thought I understood what being a Christian was all about, but being with your Paul's Marks," the name always made him smile. "Well, there's something different about them, about you. An assurance, I don't have."

"Really Brad. I thought you were a Christian?"

"So did I. I try to keep the Ten Commandments-- most of them anyway. I regularly attend church. I even go to a Christian college. I didn't question it until lately. It's just that being with Josh and the others..."

Jeanette had never heard such hesitancy in Brad before. "It's Jesus Christ," she told him. "Being a

Christian has nothing to do with being good, Brad," she
said and smiled at his expression. "Being a Christian has
everything to do with accepting what Jesus did for us by
dying on the cross and rising again for us."

"You really believe He did all those things? Rev.
Weathersby says all that is just a metaphor, and that it
didn't really happen. He says Jesus was simply a good
man, and we're to try to be kind like He was."

"But Jesus himself claimed to be God and
documents back up His claim. Brad, either Jesus was a
liar, deliberately trying to deceive people, a lunatic who
didn't know better or exactly who He said He was. If he
was a liar or a lunatic, he was not a good man. The only
logical choice then, is that Jesus Christ was and is
exactly who He said He was.

"Have you...or do you want to accept Jesus as your
savior, Brad?"

Brad was silent for a long moment. "You've given
me a lot to think about, Jeanette."

Jeanette turned away in disappointment. Reaching
over, he gave her a quick hug. "I didn't say no, Darling,
but it is a big step. What you say sounds good, but what
Rev. Weathersby says also makes a good case. Give me
time to think, all right."

An edge of excitement hovered. Maybe, thought
Jeanette, this is why God brought us together.

The smile she threw Brad was bright with promise.

His charm quickly won over her father and mother,
and long into the night her father and Brad talked.
Jeanette had taken her upbringing for granted. Now, she

glimpsed the depth of her father's Biblical knowledge and understanding and was glad he could answer Brad's astute questions.

Coming into her room late Saturday night, her mother burst her bubble of happiness. "Jeanette, Brad is a nice young man."

Jeanette eyes shown with a self-confidence she had not felt since before her engagement. "I know, Mom. I'm so glad you like him."

As though she needed to occupy her hands, Mrs. Roberts smoothed the counterpane on the bed. "I do like him, Jeanette, so does your father."

Jeanette sat down facing her mother. "But what? What's wrong with him?" She sensed her mother's disappointment.

"I think you know. As nice as Brad is, he does not have a solid commitment to Christ."

"But he's a Christian, Mom, just mixed up."

"Is he?" Sitting down beside her daughter, Mrs. Roberts told her, "Are you going to be unequally yoked, not just with an unbeliever, but maybe with someone not as committed to Christ as you are? It's something to seriously consider."

"Brad is searching, Mom, I do know that, and I am concerned." Jeanette pursed her lips.

"I also know I made a commitment to marry Brad...and I do love him," she defended herself.

With tender compassion, Mrs. Roberts smoothed away a lock of her daughter's short hair. "Did you cut your hair to please Brad? I know you always liked your hair long."

Jeanette wondered at her mother's s abrupt change of thought. "Brad thought this more sophisticated. It's also easy to maintain on a daily basis, but the perms cost a fortune. Thankfully, I don't need those too often."

"You trust Brad with something as important to you as your physical image. Are you willing to trust your Heavenly Father with your spiritual image?" She quoted Jeanette's verse, emphasizing as she did so, "Trust in the Lord with all your heart; and lean not unto your own understanding," She continued with the next verse, "In all your ways acknowledge him, and he will direct your paths."

The conversation whirled about in Jeanette's mind long after she retired. Silently, she defended her position. "He is searching. He will come to know Christ the way I do." Finally, "Besides, I love Brad, and I made a commitment."

The phrase became her litany as the days passed. Yet part of the verse from Proverbs continued to haunt her 'lean not unto your own understanding', your own understanding. But being faithful and staying committed wasn't her idea. God was directing her paths, wasn't he? Doubt crept in, and Jeanette determined to find the answer to her doubts.

It had been a good weekend despite her mother's gentle reminders. The sun had been warm with just a hint of chill in the air, allowing the younger members of the family to play outside. The family members of grandparents and aunts and uncles and cousins gathering for the huge turkey dinner accepted Brad without hesitation. Of course, Brad was used to fitting into any social situation. Jeanette couldn't help but be proud to stand beside him or to meet his gaze across the crowded room throughout the afternoon.

However, after her mother's talk, she was glad to return to school, away from the questioning eyes of her mother. In time, her mother would understand. Brad would come around. She would see to it Brad really understood.

Unfortunately, once back at school, Brad reverted to his former disinterest and condescension, leaving Jeanette both frustrated and angry.

Then the movie was released.

CHAPTER FIFTEEN:

The weekend after thanksgiving, the weather turned cold. Jeanette bundled up in navy wool slacks, navy and cream ski sweater and her warm coat, boots and hat. She pulled on her gloves as they left the building.

"Have you heard about the new movie in town?" Darilyn asked as they met after a mid-morning class. Snow crunched under their feet as they walked across the campus.

"What movie?" Jeanette laughed. "I don't know when I've last been to one. Not too many of them interest me these days, not with all the sex and violence."

"That's just it." Darilyn turned and walked backwards so she could face her friend. "This movie has the usual amount of that and more. I guess it is really obscene. Josh says it's pornographic."

Jeanette stared at her friend. "Josh. You're not saying he saw it."

"Of course not silly. But he read about it at a website that reviews the latest movies, books and stuff. Even the secular reviewers are panning it for its gratuitous sex and violence." She hurried on. "Josh said his dad plans to lead a protest against the Theater-Three downtown for showing it. "We're..."

Jeanette grabbed her as she stumbled. "I think you'd better watch where you're going, Dari. Now what's all this about?"

"Josh, thought,"

Jeanette smiled. These days it was Josh this, Josh that. It was almost a replay of Sandie before the wedding. She regretted not seeing Sandie over the Thanksgiving Holiday but between spending time with her family, and Sandie splitting her time between two family gatherings, there had been little time to get together other than for a few minutes after church when she introduced Brad. Sandie had been radiant with her happiness, and it was obvious she adored her new husband, as he adored her.

Jealousy tugged at Jeanette now as it did then. As much as she cared for Brad, she knew their relationship was based on respect rather than overwhelming passion--at least on her part. She corrected herself. The way Brad had been acting lately, that respect might be mainly on her part. His condescension hurt more than ever. Once more, he tried to get her to buy a designer wedding gown, as well as go to Wichita with his mother to purchase clothes at an exclusive shop.

He was not overly understanding when she told him firmly she could not afford such an expenditure. She heard rumors, too, he was seeing Tony, though he passed this off with such ardency, Jeanette believed him--at the time.

He had been so sincere in his search at Thanksgiving, Jeanette found herself pushing him to a decision. He responded by flatly refusing to attend the Wednesday youth group meetings with her. At her fervent pleas, Brad grew sullen and irritable, while Jeanette responded with frustration and anger. At night, she continued to search for answers with a heart filled with stubborn determination. She would bring Brad around. She would make their relationship work. But the harder she tried, the further apart they seemed to get.

"Jeanette, Jeanette," Darilyn called as she snapped her fingers in front of her friend's face. "Are you with me?"

Jeanette jumped back to the present. "Ah, you were talking about the movie."

"Yes, Josh thought Paul's Marks could jump on this one. After all, it's young adults that Hollywood tries to capture. We'll show them differently. Are you with us?"

Once more, Brad refused to attend, so head high, Jeanette attended the meeting with Darilyn who picked her up.

A huge movie poster met her as she followed Darilyn down the stairs into the large octagonal youth room. She blanched as she stared at the half-clothed picture of her sister, Cynthia.

Her knees shaking, she sat down in the last row of folding chairs and closed her eyes. "Please God, please don't let anyone know she's my sister."

The enthusiasm with which the others tackled plans to boycott, write letters, and picket the movie theater precluded them from noticing Jeanette's unusual silence.

Pleading a very real pounding headache, Jeanette asked Darilyn to take her home early.

Tears thickening her throat, Jeanette gulped out the news to her shocked aunt and uncle. For the first time in her life, Jeanette really and truly hated her sister. If Brad ever found out about Cynthia...

The organized youth group made the papers, and Brad was less than pleased when Jeanette carried a picket sign. With his stinging disapproval in her ears, Jeanette found little to celebrate when the theater decided not to run the movie.

By Christmas time, Jeanette felt only relief at leaving McFadden and Brad to go home. Without Brad's dominating presence, Jeanette relaxed and her laughter returned. Shaking her head at herself, she tried to put things into perspective. Brad only did what he thought best for her. He was good for her.

"Lord," she prayed, "Brad is every girl's dream. Guess I'm just not used to his life-style yet. It seems so shallow."

She sighed, "But I've given him my word, I just have to try harder to make it work. Make it work, Lord. Make it work. Help Him turn to you."

It wasn't until Jeanette glimpsed the six-foot pine in the high ceiling living room, decorated with an eclectic collection of ornaments that the wonder and awe of the Christmas season surrounded her. She fingered the ornaments: the antique gold bulb handed down mother to daughter for three generations; the three birds left of the blue bird of happiness collection her father gave her mother their first Christmas together; the plaster ornament with her own hand print and third grade picture. Each decoration brought back sweet, poignant memories.

She brushed tears from her eyes as her engagement ring flashed in the twinkling tree lights. Her wedding! This time next year she would be Mrs. Brad Marsden. The thought of spending Christmas with his family made her shiver.

December in Brad's circle had been nothing but a series of receptions and parties she attended with Brad. Liquor flowed at some of the parties, and Jeanette often felt isolated and alone while Tony Sornborg sparkled. Her pitying glance did nothing to build Jeanette's self-confidence.

Before returning home, she attended a small business party at the Marsden's elegant home, mansion, actually, Jeanette thought. Decorated with taste and a formal style only money could buy, Jeanette longed for her comfortable home. Even the tree, standing tall and straight covered with a precise balance of blue lights and flocking, left her cold.

Though the wealth of packages under the tree proclaimed abundance, Jeanette knew no amount of casually purchased gifts could possibly mean as much as the few, but carefully chosen or handmade presents under her family's tree.

For the first time, Jeanette truly appreciated her home, her parents' traditions.

After the usual Swedish traditional supper of Swedish meatballs, mashed potatoes, peas, and rice pudding, and after her father read the Christmas story from Luke 2, Jeanette and her parents reverently knelt around the tree. Love filled her heart and spread, blocked only by her negative feelings for her sister.

Surrounded by her laughing father and secretive mother, Jeanette opened the few gifts addressed to her. Already, she sported the "Trust God" pin Sandie had given her earlier in the afternoon. She held up a shelf unit, carefully crafted by her father, and boots she knew cost her mother dear. The purse she'd picked out for her mother, delighted her mother as the tools her uncle helped her pick out, did her father.

Finally, one small package remained under the brightly decorated tree.

"For me?" she asked as her father dropped it into her lap. "What is this?"

"Came in the mail for you," her mother answered, adding, "Open it, dear."

Quickly, Jeanette unwrapped the package, opened the small ornate box. Gasping, she held up a beautiful blue sapphire ring. Slipping it onto her finger she found it a perfect fit. Brad? But no, he'd already given her an expensive designer jacket.

"Who's it from, Jean?"

With shaking fingers, Jeanette picked up the card and read silently. "Sorry for losing what meant so much to you and must have cost a great deal. My thoughts and prayers go with you, John."

Jeanette gulped back her tears. How could she have so misjudged him? She well knew, he could ill afford such an expense. He had cared, cared very much! Though she had scorned him and turned to Brad, he still prayed for her--and was not ashamed to admit it.

Jeanette tried to picture Brad admitting such vulnerability, but could not. Any discussion about a personal God left him uncomfortable and her frustrated. But, of course, Brad would change eventually. He was searching...

Smiling through tears, Jeanette choked out an explanation. "J...John must have felt it necessary to replace my class ring he lost."

She broke down at the caring, if questioning, expression on the faces of her parents, confiding her doubts about her engagements while assuring them she would see it through.

"Jean," her mother said, "remember God loves you and wants what is best for you. If you really want to know God's will, ask Him. He will make it clear, but you have to be willing to listen."

"Don't worry Mom, Dad, I know things will come out right, I know it." She didn't want them to think she was going to walk out on her commitment. Not her!

But, despite her assurances to her concerned parents, Jeanette, was not sure, not sure at all.

CHAPTER SIXTEEN:

Following the Christmas--New Year break, Jeanette found herself looking forward to returning to school and to Brad. After all her prayers, she was sure things would be different once they talked things out. She recalled how sincere Brad had been, and his penetrating questions to her father during the Thanksgiving Holiday. She prayed Brad read the new Bible she gave him at Christmas. He had promised to read it, though reluctantly. She even dared hope that he had made a commitment during the school Christmas break.

Brad missed her as she had missed him, and she reveled in the strength of his arms about her, his hungry kisses. Shakily, she pulled away from him, "Brad, have you been reading your new Bible."

His arms dropped to his side. "Let's not get started on that now?"

"But did you?"

"Yes, Jeanette, I did. I have faithfully read something every day. Happy?" he pulled her close and sighed when her eyes brightened not with passion, but with the missionary zeal she knew he'd come to detest.

"Have you made a commitment?

"Not yet. Give me time, Darling. All right? Time."
He covered her mouth with his own. For his sake, she

quelled her disappointment and gave herself up to his embrace.

Later, she hesitantly showed him the ring she received from John. His eyes darkened with anger, and he jerked it from her finger. "I'll not have you wearing another man's ring."

"But he just gave it to me to replace my class ring, and I like it," she protested. She grabbed for it, but he held it out of her reach and stuck it into his pocket.

"I'll give it back, promise."

"When," Jeanette asked stubbornly.

He surveyed her with some exasperation. "You are the most stubborn woman I have ever come across. When you get an idea in that pretty head of yours, you just don't let go, do you?"

Jeanette flushed. It angered her to hear from Brad almost the same thing she had heard from her father over the vacation, even to the same inflection of voice. That had been a minor thing, but this. Tears stung her eyes.

Seeing her tears, Brad softened. Putting a finger under her chin, he lifted her face to his. Very gently, he kissed her soft lips. "I'll give it back real soon, trust me."

She nodded.

To her consternation, he had it appraised. "It's worth three times or more the cost of that silly ring he lost. Probably still trying to make points with you." His smile had more than a hint of smirk. "Too late for him, you belong to me." He dropped the ring into Jeanette's waiting hand.

"I want you to return it to him immediately. You will have nothing more to do with him." He paused, adding, "And don't tell anyone else about this. I will not be laughed at behind my back. My fiancée, accepting a ring from my rival."

Jeanette blushed, John, Brad's rival? Hardly, though she wished... Jeanette refused to complete the traitorous thought. Brad's possessiveness irritated her, but she held her peace.

She did not send the ring back. Not only was the ring a replacement for her class ring, but she also could not hurt John further by refusing his gift. When she looked at it, it reminded her of John's prayers for her, and she felt a certain measure of comfort.

She did send him a polite note of thank you, adding. "Thank you for praying for me. It is a great comfort."

The ring she put in a small coin purse and hid in her top drawer, only to take it out again and again. It brought back so many memories of John, his laughter, his teasing smile, his sensitivity...at times, and, most of all, the bond they had in their Christian walk. Too late, she began to understand the depth of her feelings for John. Too late.

Her sad realization made it difficult to hide her growing disillusionment with Brad and increased her desire to have that kind of bond with him.

At night, she cried out, "Lord, please let Brad accept you. I don't understand. The harder I try, the more he fights against you."

The strain of their relationship exhausted her, not to mention her classes, studies, and his social engagements that took up more and more of the weekends. Added to her already over burdened schedule were meetings with his mother, who more and more took over the wedding plans.

Both her aunt and uncle lovingly begged her to slow down, but she did not see how that was even possible. She found respite in the quiet of the sanctuary on Sundays, and in the joyous worship and fun of Paul's Marks, though it hurt that Brad continued to evade her attempts to get him to, once more, attend with her.

The more she pushed, the more condescending and arrogant Brad became. An emptiness gnawed at Jeanette, and anger--an anger she knew she could not allow to show. Not if she wanted Brad to see her as a Christian witness. The effort was tiring.

She was surprised to see her father waiting for her when she arrived home from school Wednesday afternoon. She had finished her last test and was thinking ahead to her date that evening with Brad, a sort of last outing before she went home for Easter break.

"Dad," his silent embrace concerned her. Had he forgotten, Brad planned to drive her home the next day.

"Dad?" she asked again, seeing the paleness of his face. "What's wrong...Mom?"

"No, Jeanette. It's Cynthia; she's home."

Jeanette closed her eyes so her father would not see the sudden flash of anger. What had her dear sister done now? Another thought hit. Brad! Oh no! She couldn't have Brad know about her sister.

"You knew Brad was planning to drive me home in the morning, Dad, so why...."

He cut her off. "Jeanette, Cynthia is dying."

Her mouth suddenly went dry. "No. Cynthia, you're sure." All the evil things she had thought about her sister flickered through her mind like a bad movie print.

Her dad started to speak, stopped, cleared his throat. "I came to get you, so we can all have as much time as possible together, before..." He stopped, cleared his throat again. "Anyway, she's been asking for you."

The ride home was long and silent, giving Jeanette ample time to think back to when she and Cynthia were little girls together. She admired her older sister then. Cynthia had always been so full of life and quite the ham. Back then, Jeanette remembered sitting on the wooden gate of the corral as the adoring audience, while Cynthia pranced about the corral, acting out one of the plays she had memorized.

Adoration turned to dislike, disillusionment, and hate. Jeanette bit her lip. Some Christian she was, hating her own sister.

"Help me, Lord," she breathed quietly, "help me love Cynthia again. Regardless of what she has done." She wished someone was there to hold her hand. Her mind flashed to John first, then Brad.

"Your sister. I didn't know you had a sister, Darling." Brad responded when she phoned him with the news. "Do you want me to drive down tomorrow anyway?" She heard the edginess in his tone.

"No, that's not necessary," she said wearily.

He sounded relieved. " I'll see you when you get back. If you need anything…"

"I may be late coming back, and I have appointments...the wedding."

Brad waved all that aside. "Don't worry about a thing, Darling. Mother can take over. I'm sure she'll have things well in hand by the time you return."

"I'll just bet she will," Jeanette muttered as she hung up. She felt her dream wedding slipping through her fingers. The more she and Mrs. Marsden planned, the less and less Jeanette felt needed at her own wedding.

Clenching her teeth, she put her irritation and frustration over the wedding aside. Cynthia was her concern now.

There was no way to hide her shock when she walked into Cynthia's bedroom, the largest one in the house, accessible from both kitchen and living room. Red and pink roses trailed up and down the wall paper, faded now from years of sun beaming through the large window overlooking the front drive and the barn. Cynthia lay in the waterbed her parents had given her when she graduated from high school, but had never taken with her.

The beautiful eyes that mirrored her own were glazed with pain. The smooth cheeks pale and sunken.

The usually petulant mouth, however, held a soft smile. "Jeanette." Cynthia's eyes brightened, and she held out a thin hand. "I'm so glad you are here."

Jeanette sucked in a breath. How could this shrunken tired woman be her vivacious sister?

"Cynthy," she whispered, reverting to her childhood name for her sister, "what happened?"

CHAPTER SEVENTEEN:

Taking her sister's hand, Jeanette sat down on the rosebud comforter, covering the double bed with its black, wrought-iron headboard. Plastering on a false smile, Jeanette tried to ignore the medicinal smell of the room, the smell of disease...and death.

"No, Sis, don't try to put on a cheery face for me. I know the truth." Cynthia's smile was a travesty. She fought for breath. "I'm glad you came."

For a long moment, Cynthia basked in her sister's presence as though getting up the courage to speak. "Jeanette, I have so much to say to you." A coughing spell frightened Jeanette.

Leaping to her feet, she ran for her mother. Mrs. Roberts had worked as a nurse's aid for a time many years earlier, and Jeanette trusted she knew what to do.

Her mother firmly closed the bedroom door, leaving Jeanette outside, more frightened than she'd ever been in her life. She had never really lost anyone close to her before. Her mother's father died before she was born, and her father's mother when she was three, too young to remember.

Death had not touched her personally. She thought of Cynthia and her wasted life. Running to her own room, Jeanette flung herself on her knees beside her bed.

"Lord, you can't take Cynthia away now. Lord, she's my sister...and, and, she doesn't know you, and and, she is young...and, and." Even to her own ears, Jeanette's reasons sounded weak. Why should God spare her sister who might very well be reaping what she herself had sown?

Jeanette shuddered, thinking of her sister's shrunken face. How could she have gotten so ill, and so quickly? Maybe her dad was mistaken. Now that Cynthia was home, she knew her parents would do everything in their power to take care of their daughter.

Jeanette's heart smote her anew with conviction. She had begun to hate her sister and for what--fear her friends would discover the seductive actress was her sister? Resting her head on her bed, Jeanette saw the truth. She was afraid, all right, afraid her Christian friends would not accept her if they knew. Brad. She trembled to think of his response.

"Lord, forgive me. Forgive me for my pride concerning my own sister. Forgive my arrogant attitude toward her." Tears trickling down her cheeks, Jeanette continued to pour out her heart in a way she had not done for a long time.

"Jeanette." The gentle hand on her shoulder startled her, and she turned around.

"Mother. Cynthia, is she?"

"All right for now."

"Thanks Lord," she whispered. Getting up, she took the tissue her mother handed her and wiped her face.

"Father said, said..." She could not say the dreaded
word."

"Cynthia has cancer."

Jeanette's eyes brightened with hope. "But cancer
can be treated."

Mrs. Roberts, took her daughter's arm and sat with
her on the bed. "Jeanette, Cynthia has already been
through much treatment."

"Then she's getting better."

"No, Jeanette. She came home because there is
nothing anyone can do for her." For a moment, her
mother remained silent. "Cynthia knew about the
diagnoses just before she came home last summer."

"Why didn't she tell us about it?" Jeanette cried,
wishing she could take back some of her hard thoughts
about her sister.

"She wasn't ready yet. But that's why she left Tony
as she did."

"It was cruel."

"Yes, but she cared enough to leave him. You see,
she has a very fast-acting cancer. She went into
treatment, but it did little good." Her mother stopped,
unable to continue.

Jeanette's shoulders slumped. "She's really going to
die then."

"Unless God chooses to heal her."

"Of course, we can get everyone to pray for her."
Jeanette was off and running. "We can call the church. I

can call Rev. Connors and ask him to mobilize Paul's Marks..."

Mrs. Roberts laid a restraining hand on her daughter's arm. "That is a good idea. Prayer is the only answer, but, Jeanette, I want you to be prepared for whatever answer God gives us."

"God does heal."

"Yes, and He will heal Cynthia. While He may chose to heal her physical body and give her a long life here." She struggled for words. "Jean dear, the Lord might want to take your sister home with Him. That too is healing."

Jeanette stared at her mother. "Cynthia! Mom, she has flatly denied Christ. You know that, if she dies, she'll. She'll...go to hell," Jeanette whispered.

Putting an arm around her daughter, Mrs. Roberts held her close. Jeanette sensed her mother needed her as much as she needed her mother. "Jeanette," he mother choked, continued. "Your sister has come home in more ways than one."

"Mom, are you telling me, Cynthia has accepted Jesus Christ as her savior. How? When? Oh, Mom."

"I'm not going to spoil things for her. She wants to tell you herself. When she's feeling up to it, you can talk to her again."

Impatiently, Jeanette waited for Cynthia to wake up. She helped her mother bake bread, releasing her frustration as she kneaded the dough. Forming it into a ball, Jeanette slammed it down on the flour-covered counter and spread it out with the palms of her hands.

She worked the yeasty smelling dough, releasing the gluten for the rising before forming it into a loaf that she set into a greased bread pan. Before she finished, six loaves stood ready for the oven. The exercise had exorcised some of her frustration. After washing her flour covered hands, Jeanette put the first three loaves in the oven to bake.

She loved the warm, tangy smell of homemade bread as it baked in the oven; loved the taste of its warm freshness with real butter and honey her father bought from a neighbor who kept bees. But, she hated the wait. She recalled asking her mother when she was all of five, "Hurry it up, Mamma, I's hungry."

Her mother laughed softly. "For everything there is a time, and sometimes we have to wait for the right time. It isn't time to eat the bread right now. It is time to wait."

She had never learned to wait well.

The rays of the evening sun touched the snow-covered steps to the back porch, and she had just taken out the last loaves of bread from the oven when her mother told her Cynthia was awake and waiting for her.

Taking in a deep breathe, Jeanette opened the door and walked into her sister's room, the room they had shared as children when they wanted to whisper secrets to each other in the dark. Now the darkness was in her heart, and she gulped back tears at seeing her vital sister so weak.

"Cynthia?" Jeanette entered hesitantly, staring at the far wall with its picture of Jesus in the garden praying.

Her sister had hated the picture, but her parents insisted it stay.

"I'm glad they made me keep it."

Her sister's eyes on the picture, Jeanette studied her sister's face. Gone was the petulance, the hardness in the eyes. Gone, the heavy make up and too-red lips. The face turning toward her was soft and kind, the face she recalled from her childhood. "Do you remember when I used to force you to sit on the corral gate and listen to me parrot lines?"

"You didn't have to force me," Jeanette said with a smile. The years dropped away, and, with them, Jeanette's awkwardness with this new-old sister. They upstaged each other recalling incidents from their childhood, setting them both giggling like little girls again.

Cynthia's choking cough brought Jeanette sharply back to the present. They were not children any longer, and her sister, her only sister, was dying. Tears stung her eyes. She blinked them away, but they insisted on gathering at the corners of her eyes and dripping onto the full sleeve of the vertically striped blue and white blouse she wore over matching blue slacks.

Cynthia held her hand. "Sis, it's all right to cry."

"I love you Cynthy," the words poured out unpremeditated as love for her sister flowed over Jeanette. It no longer mattered what her sister had done, or not done. She loved her. How like her Heavenly Father's love for them, she thought.

"I love you too, Sis. I'm just sorry I failed you. Failed Mom and Dad." Cynthia bit her lip, a habit so like her younger sister's. "And failed God."

"Mom said..." Jeanette stopped, remembering Cynthia wanted to tell the news herself.

"You know then, that I have come home." For a moment, she closed her eyes, and Jeanette was unsure whether to stay or leave when Cynthia opened them again. "I have no excuse. Like all our family, I was stubborn and wanted my own way. I got tired of trying to listen to God and even more tired of trying to obey Him. I wanted to be like my friends. I seemed like such a prude beside them. I thought they were having fun." She shook her head.

"It's so easy to be fooled when we close our minds and ears to what God is really saying to us. The things I did even in high school. You would be ashamed of me."

Jeanette's cheeks colored, paled. She had been ashamed of her sister, bitterly ashamed. "Cynthia, you don't have to tell any of this. I haven't been so wonderful myself." She hesitated before continuing, "I have been ashamed of you, and been afraid to admit to my friends that Cynthia Harvey the actress in that awful movie was my sister."

"I don't blame you, but if you think you need my forgiveness, you have it. I can't make up for all the hurt I caused you and the folks, even poor Tony, but I can say," a smile lit her face as she continued, "I, too, have been forgiven. Jesus has forgiven me. It was so easy... I asked. I wanted so much fame, fortune, love. What I found was poverty of spirit, emptiness and shallow relationships instead of love. It took this, this cancer to make me see the truth."

"But, but you're dying."

A soft light touched her sister's face, "Oh, but Sis, I have only just begun to really live. If God chooses not to heal me, I'm ready to go. Just think, Jeanette, I'll be waiting for you on the other side. I'll be waiting for my little Sis."

Cynthia fought for breath, and Jeanette started to get up, but Cynthia's hand on her arm stopped her. "Sis, remember to always listen to Him. Don't stubbornly go your own way...it is...not...worth...it. God's way is best. Trust Him." Her violent coughing sprung Jeanette into action.

"Mom," she called, rushing into the kitchen, "Cynthia."

It was a day, Jeanette long remembered. An afternoon of love and memory and an evening of deep searing pain. Soon after her coughing spell, Cynthia rallied, but all knew it was just a matter of time. Cynthia said good-bye to her family who waited by her bedside. With infinite tenderness, Tony held her hand, his face anguished at losing another woman he loved. The pastor, too, waited, prayed.

Five minutes passed eleven, Cynthia slipped peacefully into the presence of her Lord.

With the funeral, Jeanette returned to school a week late. Her Uncle Silas and Aunt Evelyn, who came out for the funeral, drove her back to school. She was grateful for their sensitivity in leaving her to her own thoughts as she curled up in the back seat deep in her own grief.

Easter for her would ever after remind her of her sister's death and her triumph of life with Christ. But then, wasn't that what Easter was all about, Jesus' victory over sin and death?

Brad called, awkwardly conveying his condolences. When he excused himself from attending the funeral, Jeanette found herself resenting the huge spray of red roses he sent, needing more than words, more than a token for her wounded heart.

Jeanette also worried about leaving her folks to deal with their grief. She would have stayed longer had they not insisted she finish out the year. But her coveted goal of graduating hardly seemed important now.

Still, somehow, she must struggle through; must make her parents proud. She thought too of Brad. Death was real now to her, eternal life as well. Something stirred within her heart, but she had no time to listen, not with her mind filled with dread for Brad. Somehow, she must make Brad understand his need to make a commitment to Christ.

No longer would she be silent.

CHAPTER EIGHTEEN:

Brad's fist crashed down on the arm of the flowered love seat he shared with Jeanette "Enough all ready, Jeanette." His stiff arm sliced the air near his throat. "I am fed up with being preached at."

Brad's eyes flashed, and his body tensed with anger at her latest onslaught. Fear sliced down Jeanette's spine. She must make him see the truth.

She glanced about the Marsden family living room, trying to calm her racing heart. The soft spring greens of the carpet and curtains echoed in the textured flowers on the early American couch, love seat and twin wing-back chairs. To her left a charcoal gray fireplace crackled as flames leaped up, sending warmth, but little light into the room. The mantel held heirloom cups and figurines, and over the mantel hung a Scottish coat of arms. The room done with taste, elegance and style, promoted a tranquility Jeanette could not appreciate at the moment.

"Brad, you have to understand."

"No," he thundered, causing her to shrink back from his fury, "you need to understand. I am not marrying a zealot who thinks I'm not good enough for her. I am marrying a woman who is willing to listen and obey me." His lips twisted. "As old fashioned as it may be, I expect loving obedience from my wife."

His gaze speared her. "That Bible you quote so glibly says a wife is to respect her husband and to submit to his authority, does it not?"

A soft flush on her cheeks, Jeanette slowly nodded.

"Tell me Jeanette, will you be able to submit to my authority once we're married, when you refuse to do so now?"

"But," Jeanette protested, "we're not married yet. If you will just accept Christ..."

"As you have asked, pleaded, threatened and argued about since you returned from your sister's funeral." Sighing, Brad leaned back and stared across the room to the armoire hiding a complete media center behind its early American decor.

"I know you're hurting, Jeanette. I can understand that. I can also understand your concern for my eternal destiny that you believe to be the deepest, darkest part of hell."

He continued despite Jeanette's protest. "What you cannot seem to do, my stubborn little darling, is accept me as I am. If Christ accepts me as I am, why can't you?"

The thrust hit home. "Oh, Brad," Jeanette cried as tears gathered in her eyes. "I...I just wanted...tried."

Wrapping an arm about her shoulders, Brad's countenance softened. "I know what you want Jeanette, but I'm not ready yet."

"At Thanksgiving you seemed so close to really committing your life to Christ. What happened?"

Brad rubbed her shoulder before answering quietly. "You."

Pushing away, Jeanette stared up at him in consternation. "Me! But I just..."

"Badgered and badgered me about the whole thing, never letting me sort things out for myself. Jeanette, I will not be pushed into anything, and you don't want me to say I made some commitment just to make you happy, do you?"

Jeanette shook her head, her heart heavy with self-recrimination. "But the Bible says not to be unequally yoked. Brad, I thought you were a Christian when I agreed to marry you."

"Now you are sure I'm going to hell, because I don't have the same kind of commitment you do."

Jeanette bit her lip. "I...I just want to be sure."

"Are you going to turn into a nagging shrew whenever you don't like something about me? I won't have it, Jeanette. I expect respect, and I expect you to back off on this until I bring up the subject."

"But I..." Jeanette's cheeks reddened with his assault. It both angered and depressed her. Did she truly come across in that fashion?

Brad held her close. "No, no more. I am reading my Bible regularly, Darling. I do believe in Jesus Christ. More I am not ready to commit, not yet. I need time. Time to think, time to sort through the things your father explained. Time to read the books he recommended. Be patient. I will do it."

Hope lit her eyes until he added, "I will also explore the books Rev. Weathersby suggested." Seeing the light fade from her face, he questioned, "Are you afraid, my little saint, your brand of Christianity will not stand the test of rational thought?"

"Of course not," came her hot denial. At Brad's chuckle, she stared down at the toe of her boots.

"Then give me a chance." Tucking a finger under her chin, he made her face him. "Jeanette, why are you so determined to be God's little enforcer on this matter? Are you so afraid God cannot reach me without your help? What about all this trust in Him you keep talking about. You seem to have little enough where I am concerned. When or if I do totally commit my life to Christ I want it to be for the right reasons. A commitment is not to be entered into lightly, but when a commitment is made, it is for keeps."

"Fear. Trust. Commitment." Brad's comments haunted Jeanette.

Darilyn and the other members of the youth group helped her ease back into school and church activities, though for her, the excitement was gone. On campus at times, she found herself staring around at the buildings wondering where she was. Thankfully, Darilyn stuck beside her often leading her like a child through a maze of classes.

Brad, too, was there but a constraint hung between them since the night Brad confronted her. His accusations speared her heart, a heart wounded from her sister's death, but not yet ready to accept, in totality, Brad's assessment of her faith.

In response, to Brad's relief, Jeanette stopped witnessing to him. Burning with her need to have him make a firm commitment, the effort keep silent tore her apart inside. Her frustrations grew as Mrs. Marsden laid out a whole schedule of receptions and teas, showers and other social engagements all geared, thought Jeanette, to make me forget about Cynthia and turn me into a social butterfly." The thought made her shudder.

Her wedding gown hung in the large closet downstairs. Its flowing lines never failed to inspire her awe at what her hands had created. Wryly, she visualized the glowing newspaper description. "The bride's floor length white satin gown was a fairy creation of puffed sleeves, lace covered open neckline, and fitted waist. The bride wore a matching veil of soft Venetian lace. The whole designed and sewn by the bride."

Despite her attempts to keep up with her classes, Jeanette knew things were not going well. No matter how hard she tried, she just couldn't pull it all together. Not only did Jeanette struggle at school, but church no longer provided an oasis. Her mind churned with her growing frustration over not only her failure at school, but also her failure to make a difference in Brad's life. She felt like a failure at keeping even a portion of her wedding plans her own.

Mrs. Marsden had indeed taken over. She reserved First Grand for the wedding, and Rev. Weathersby to officiate, (though Jeanette insisted Rev. Connors also have his say during the ceremony).

Brad's mother's planned the reception and the guest list and about everything else, thought Jeanette, except the color scheme of blue and white and her attendants.

As much as her graduation had slipped in importance because of Cynthia, it bothered Jeanette that her wedding the Sunday afternoon after her graduation completely overshadowed the celebration.

Mrs. Marsden waved aside her objections. "My dear, many family members and others of importance are expected to attend the graduation. We cannot expect them to return again for a wedding later in the summer. Certainly your parents would find it easier to come just once, don't you think."

Biting her lip, Jeanette agreed.

Like a maze with every escape but another dead end, Jeanette felt herself trapped in circumstances she could no longer control. Her hasty prayers did little to soothe her burdened heart.

Friday, one week before graduation, Jeanette could no longer hold in the searing grief clawing her apart. Locking herself in her room, she wept. She wept out her sorrow; wept out her hurt and pain and her frustration not only over Brad's easy acceptance of her silence, but also the loss of the simple wedding of her dreams.

In a few days, her mother and father would arrive not only for the graduation, proud she had made the Dean's List with her 3.6 average. Proud. Maybe, but not Jeanette, not when she had failed to keep her grades to

the 4.0 she carried since high school. Somehow, after Cynthy's death, the words of her books swam before her eyes and the simplest of concepts escaped her. The only thing not suffering was her sewing projects, for her skillful fingers smoothed and tucked and guided the smooth material without guidance from her numbed, confused mind.

Inevitably, her thoughts turned to John and his quiet faith. Pulling out the Blue Sapphire, Jeanette slipped it onto her finger and let her mind drift. Vivid images like snap shots flashed through her mind. John at the truck stop, irritating, but still a gentleman. John slipping in beside her at church. John at the footbridge. John's deep faith and quiet trust.

His face faded, replaced by Brad's handsome countenance. Slipping off the ring, Jeanette reluctantly put it away even as she guiltily put John from her heart.

She, who held commitment so highly, betrayed her commitment to Brad in her traitorous thoughts. "Jesus, help me." she cried, throwing herself onto her bed and burying her head into her pillow. "What am I to do? What? I have failed. I cannot forget John. Yet, I made a commitment to Brad. I tried so hard at college, yet failed to keep my grade point up. I tried to win Brad to you, but he's further from you than ever."

Tears streamed down her face. "I couldn't even have my own wedding."

Jeanette wept, her body shaking as great sobs tore her.

Outside her room her uncle stopped Evelyn from entering her room. "Leave her be. She needs time alone. Time to settle things with her own heart."

"It's so hard to let her suffer alone, Silas." She let him lead her from the hall.

"I know, Evey, I know, but we must trust God to get through to her."

The evening sun threw long shadows against the house, and still the door remained locked. The supper hour passed, and Silas only shook his head when his wife inquired, "Should I bring her supper? She's bound to be hungry."

Jeanette never knew Brad called.

Stars twinkled in through her open shades, the only light in the darkened room, and still Jeanette wept and begged God for an answer.

Finally, her tears spent, Jeanette lay exhausted on the bed. Inside an emptiness needed to be filled, a wound healed, but she was powerless to help herself.

In the darkness, in the silence, Jeanette waited.

CHAPTER NINETEEN:

Verses flitted through her mind. 'The Lord preserves the faithful; He that is faithful in that which is least is faithful also in much.' Faithful? She had tried and failed.

"I tried Lord, I tried." she sighed, "I know also I made a commitment to Brad, and I will stick to it."

"What about your faithfulness to me, Jeanette? What about your trust in me! Did you trust me, Jeanette? Did you trust me for the solutions or did you try to do things your way in your timing?"

"Jeanette, remember God, not you, and certainly not me, is in control. Trust Him." She saw again the earnestness on her mother's face.

"Trust in the Lord with all your heart; and lean not unto your own understanding." The verse learned so long ago, rolled off Jeanette's tongue as it had that Christmas so long ago when she first realized she was actually going to be able to attend ProMark.

Her mother had continued, "'In all your ways acknowledge him, and he shall direct your paths.' Now if you don't forget that, my dear, you will be fine."

But she had forgotten; had forgotten when she jumped at the chance at being Brad's wife; had forgotten when she begun to hate a sister she sensed was already hurting, had forgotten when she witnessed to Brad.

No, she admitted, she had not witnessed to Brad. Maybe at first, but somewhere along the way, she stopped listening to the leading of God's Spirit. Somewhere along the way, she substituted her own way for God's. And somewhere along the way, she lost her way.

No she had not been faithful. She had failed him as surely as Cynthia, and, in her own way, been just as rebellious. That hurt most of all. For so long, she prided herself, oh yes prided herself. She saw it all now, a panorama of her last year and a half laid out before her in vivid color. How often she failed. How often she stubbornly went her own way.

For a moment, she returned to that last afternoon with her sister. Again she heard Cynthia's warning. "Sis, remember to always listen to Him. Don't stubbornly go your own way...it is...not...worth...it. God's way is best. Trust Him."

Her mother had warned her. Cynthia warned her. Even Aunt Evelyn had clearly pointed the way out of her confusion and frustration. It was confusion and frustration she brought upon herself by refusing to listen to the still small voice of the Holy Spirit within her.

The conversation played clearly on the screen of her mind. "Why do I have doubts?"

Aunt Evelyn measured her words carefully. "Doubts can be Satan's way of breaking down your resistance, but..." she raised a hand in emphasis, "but it can be God's Holy Spirit trying to speak to you."

Confusion crossed Jeanette's face. "How do I know God's will for me?"

"Ah," her aunt voiced her approval, "you're asking the right questions. There are five simple steps to knowing God's will, Jeanette."

Jeanette waited expectantly, hoping for an easy answer to her inner conflicts.

"Prayer is your key. Have you prayed about the problem until you have the assurance of God's peace and the leading of His Holy Spirit through specific Bible passages?" Jeanette swallowed, but had not interrupted her aunt.

"Have you talked over the situation with Godly men or women who can advise you wisely? And, have you taken into consideration all the pros and cons of the decision?"

Jeanette hated to admit she had not much done any of those things in making her decision to marry Brad. She had been hurting and, at the time, he offered a ready made solution to her problem.

Her aunt continued, "All of the others make little difference if your heart isn't ready to receive God's will. Obedience isn't something you do if and when you feel like it. Obedience is willingness to do what God wants you to do before you know what that is."

Obedience. Faithfulness. Trust. It was there all the time, but she had refused to listen, refused to heed. Broken, Jeanette whispered. "What do I do now, Lord? What do I do about Brad?"

The answer came. Wait. Trust. This time Jeanette was ready. "I don't want to fight you anymore, Lord Jesus. Please, take the mess I've made of my life and my witness to Brad. Help me trust you to work all things out for your glory. Amen."

A moment later, Jeanette fell into a peaceful dreamless slumber.

The next morning, a knock on the door awakened her. "Yes," she called, surprised to see she still wore her skirt and sweater.

Her aunt stopped just inside the room. "Jeanette, are you all right?"

Getting up, Jeanette smoothed down her skirt. "Oh, yes, Aunt Evelyn. I am better than I have been in a very long time."

Her aunt silently contemplated the face of her niece, that still showed traces of tears. "You made your peace."

"Yes." Biting her lip, she shook her head. "Oh, Aunt Evelyn how can one person be so stubborn?"

Her aunt's smile held a world full of hard-won wisdom. "That's what I ask myself every time I go off on my own tangent instead of waiting on the Lord's timing, or when I don't wait to find out what the Lord wants me to do." She stopped. "But I wanted to tell you, I am off to church for a special prayer meeting for Mrs. Amory. She's in the hospital again."

"John's mother? She's never really recovered from her last bout has she? Is it the same thing?"

"I don't know, but it is serious. Your uncle even had John's recruiting officer, Sergeant Pederson put in a word for hardship leave for John. He thought the Sergeant's request along with that of the doctor's should be enough to bring him home."

Jeanette's heart went out to John. "It's very serious then."

"Serious enough that her son should be here."

After her aunt left, Jeanette knelt beside the bed. Her relationship to the Lord fully restored and her trust firmly focused on him, Jeanette prayed for John and his mother. She poured out her heart, then fell silent. Listening. Waiting.

Joy bubbled up inside her at being able to release the situation into her Savior's hands, and, with the release, came deep, abiding peace.

Getting up, Jeanette grabbed her robe and shampoo and headed for a long soak in the basement bathroom.

Refreshed, Jeanette called Brad to apologize for missing their date the evening before. Sunday afternoon, she apologized again as they sat downstairs in her Uncle's home. "Brad. I'm sorry for trying to force you to a decision." She bit her lip. "I tried so hard to make you do what I believed right. Then I just kept silent, but ..."

"Your silence spoke volumes," Brad traced the curve of her cheek. "What happened, Jeanette?" He studied the new softness in her eyes. "You're different. You're not the girl I first asked to marry me, unsure of herself, nor the zealot ready to drag me to the pearly gates."

"I'm learning to listen, Brad," Jeanette said simply. "I've given it all into His hands. You were right. I wasn't trusting in God's grace, but in myself. That's over." She took his hands in her own. "There are still problems Brad. I am concerned about marrying a man who has not made a solid commitment to the Lord. That is not God's best for his children, but..." The serenity shining from her eyes caused Brad's heart to jump. "I am waiting on Him, right now."

Putting his arms around her, Brad pulled her close and lowered his mouth to hers. "That's my girl. Don't worry about a thing, it's all under control."

A warning bell sounded in Jeanette's mind at the condescension in Brad's tone. He wanted a moldable wife, Jeanette saw that clearly now. He did not understand at all.

"Brad, Brad." Jeanette pushed away from his ardent embrace. "You don't understand."

"I understand enough, Darling."

Jeanette's eyes flashed, hot words leaped to her lips. This time she bit her lip to keep from speaking as she heeded her promise to listen, to wait.

Waiting did not come easy as last minute wedding details vied for last minute tests and papers. Darilyn's dress had to be taken in, Sandie's let out as she was now expecting her first child.

Jeanette rejoiced with her friend who arrived with her husband two days before graduation, just behind her folks. Both took their luggage to the downstairs bedrooms.

"Sandie." She hugged her friend, before being enveloped into the arms of her parents.

"Mom, Dad, I'm so glad you're here." She searched their faces. "Are you all right?"

Her mother's smile sparkled through tears. "We're fine, Jean. And you?"

"I'm fine, Mom, really I am. Come on everyone, Aunt Evelyn has a small luncheon laid out in the kitchen." Taking her father's arm, she led the way.

Laughter filled the small dining room as they ate off paper plates and used paper cups so her aunt would not be overly burdened with the extra guests, and Jeanette would not need to worry about cleaning up. Even in the midst of the laughter, Jeanette felt her father's eyes upon her with a question she knew she could not answer.

In fact, the closer the wedding date came, the more worried she became. Brad alternated between sensitivity and arrogance at her apparent submission to his plans. But he still had made no commitment to the Lord, and Jeanette's worry played havoc with her hard-won peace. Patience had never been one of her primary virtues and doubts filled her mind.

The afternoon before graduation, seeing Jeanette's state of mind, Sandie and Darilyn hauled her away for luncheon. Seated on a red vinyl bench in the small booth eating chicken nuggets and a salad, Jeanette began to relax.

"Thanks you two. I guess I was getting to be a basket case. I can't believe all the things Brad's mother comes up with for me to do, or see or attend."

Sandie laughed. "Remember how I was before my wedding? All I wanted to do was elope with the man of my dreams."

A shadow crossed Jeanette's face, and Sandie contemplated her knowingly. "Still have doubts," she asked.

Darilyn's eyes widened. "Jeanette, is that true?"

Her expression weary, Jeanette nodded, determined not to let her cheeks give away her embarrassment over her growing frustration. "It will work out," she told them, but knew from their glance at each other, they were not fooled.

Sandie asked, "What are you going to do, Jeanette?"

"Wait," she told them through clenched teeth. She knew she sounded silly, but there was nothing else she could or would tell them.

Darilyn protested, but Sandie seemed to understand and steered the conversation toward Darilyn. "What are your plans after graduation?"

Darilyn smiled. "Teach, I hope. If I can get a job around McFadden."

"I thought Jeanette said you were from Blue Rapids."

"I am," she said, flashing Jeanette a conspiratorial wink.

"Darilyn is going with, I guess you can say, or is it that you have 'an understanding' with a certain young man who lives in McFadden. A certain minister's son."

This time, Darilyn blushed. Her eyes danced with excitement. "Josh almost proposed the other night, but he's not ready to get married. He still has a year of college. Then he wants to go on to get his masters in business and computers." She sighed, a long deep sigh. "I'll have to wait forever."

"It's worth it," Sandie told her firmly, "to wait for the right one."

The question rang in Jeanette's mind. Was she marrying the right one?

Despite her tight schedule, Jeanette made time to slip away to see Mrs. Amory. The frail woman delighted in her short visits, but Jeanette knew the woman's health was not improving. It was as though she but waited for the return of her son, which had been delayed for some reason known only to the military.

Graduation dawned slightly overcast. After checking the weather report, Uncle Silas flipped off the television. "They say it's going to clear up," he told them.

For once, the report proved accurate and promptly at two o'clock Jeanette, Brad, and Darilyn walked up the aisle with their classmates for their graduation. The day, her day had finally arrived. For years, Jeanette strove toward this goal; for years, she anticipated getting a teaching degree so she might help other girls gain self confidence by learning the skills that came so naturally to her. Yet the diploma scorched her hands. Her cheeks flushed and paled by turns and anger burned inside her as her conversation with Brad, when they waited to walk down the aisle, her for her Bachelors and he for his masters degree, replayed again and again through her mind.

Her eyes sparkled with excitement and happiness as she waited beside Brad. Gowned in her long robe of blue, she let him take her hand. "Excited about the graduation, or the wedding night?" At his mocking leer, red chased across her cheeks.

"Stop it, Brad." She could hardly tell him, she tried to steer her thoughts away from their coming intimacy. "I have wanted to teach for so long. Now I'll have the chance."

At his frown, she stuttered. "Is something wrong?"

"You're going to be my wife, Darling. Quite frankly, I have no intention of sharing my wife with a class full of little brats. At least, not for sometime." His meaning was clear, and Jeanette's blush deepened.

" I have always wanted to teach," she whispered as another dream crumbled.

Brad tried to draw her stiff body into his embrace. "Don't worry, Darling, Mother will keep you busy with volunteer activities. Good for..."

"The Marsden image," Jeanette repeated bitterly, turning away.

Silently, she breathed, Please, Lord, what am I to do. This is wrong. I know this wrong, but how can I call off the wedding now?

That evening, after the graduation celebration ended, Jeanette found a letter on the desk in her room. Picking it up, she turned it over in her hands. No return address revealed the sender. Neither was there a stamp or postmark. Thinking the envelope contained another graduation greeting, Jeanette slit it opened and took out the letter.

Folding open the single sheet of typing paper, she sat down heavily onto the bed. John, the letter was from John!

CHAPTER TWENTY:

Slowly Jeanette read the letter wondering how it had
been delivered to the house. Had John himself come and
found her gone? Her heart ached within her. How she
wanted to see his teasing smile again, but no...she was to
be married in two days time.

Dear Jeanette,

Congratulations on your graduation and upcoming
marriage. I wish you only the best. I do have one
request. Would you meet me by the footbridge,
tomorrow afternoon at five? I need to see you one last
time. Will you do this for me?

Your friend in Christ,

How could she refuse? It was a small enough thing
to do. Once again, confusion swirled in Jeanette's mind,
but this time she knew where to turn. Getting on her
knees beside the bed, Jeanette laid the letter out before
the Lord.
    "Lord, I give this up to you. What do you want me to
do? Should I meet John? I know Brad wouldn't like it,
yet I feel an obligation to John somehow." She waited
then, silent, still. Images flashed through her mind of

her, of Brad, of John. In the silence, she finally accepted the truth. She had gotten into her situation when she ran ahead of God's plan for her life.

Even when she got things straightened out with her Lord, one problem remained--Brad. She knew the verses from II Corinthians 6:14 & 15, Be ye not unequally yoked together with unbelievers: for what fellowship hath righteousness with unrighteousness? and what communion hath light with darkness?

Yet she was committed to marrying him, wasn't she? For the first time, Jeanette discerned the difference in her commitments and the Lord's. She had not yet married Brad or taken vows to stay together 'for better or worse.'

'Be ye not unequally yoked together.' Brad had not yet made a commitment to the Lord. 'Be ye not unequally yoked together.'

The bedcover brushed her wet cheek. "Lord," Jeanette whispered, trying not to think about the cost of the church, the reception hall, the caterers, the wedding gifts that had been piling up at Brad's house for a week already. She tried not to think of the mocking laughter on Tony's face, or the hurt on the faces of her folks. "Lord, help me do what's right. Give me the courage to be honest with Brad."

The next morning, Jeanette related John's request to Brad. She had planned out what to say, but Brad's reaction tore her carefully rehearsed speech from her mind.

Brad's tone cut."You aren't going."

"Why not," Jeanette challenged. Until that moment she had still been undecided about what to do.

"Because I say so, that's why."

"He just wants to talk."

Brad blew up then. "How dare you expose me and my family to gossip on the morning before our wedding. What kind of girl are you anyway? I can never figure you out. One minute, you're soft and yielding, the next you're off on some tangent of your own. If I had known you had this stubborn bent..."

"What Brad Marsden?" Jeanette's eyes flashed.

He backed up hastily, "This is about John, Darling. As my bride I forbid you to see him."

"Not yet Brad."

Something in her quiet assertion angered him. "John, always John. Have you been corresponding secretly all along? I suppose you kept the ring, too."

Jeanette's cheeks flushed with anger. "How dare you, Brad. Yes, I kept the ring. I had every right to do so, and you know it. John bought it to replace my class ring, and I was not about to insult him by returning it.

"As to corresponding with John. I did write, once to apologize for hurting his feelings, and once to thank him for the ring. But even if I had, what difference would that make? I do not belong to you Brad Marsden, and I don't think I ever care to!" The words slipped out before she could recall them. Her hand flew up to hide her hot cheeks.

This is not the way she planned to end things at all. Again she felt the guilt of failure. "Oh, Brad, I didn't

mean. I did, but not...this way. Brad, I'm sorry, so
sorry."

Brad blanched, his anger gone. "It's out now, isn't it,
the truth. It's been a long time in coming, hasn't it?"

Jeanette brushed tears from her eyes, "I am truly
sorry, Brad. I tried, I really tried, but we, us together. It
was wrong from the beginning, but I was so confused. I
am not the girl you thought you were getting."

"And I am not the spiritual giant you want."
Ruefully, he fingered a lock of the hair she had let grow
since Easter break. "I know you tried. I had hoped..." He
sighed, "I should have realized....our backgrounds and
all. No offense. Love is not enough for you, is it?"

Remorse showed in her eyes. "I do love you, Brad,
but not the way a woman should love the man she's
going to spend the rest of her life with. I don't care
about your wealth or your family connections. I don't
care about status or social climbing."

As she tried to explain, the words formed almost of
their own volition. "I wanted to be loved and accepted
for myself, Brad, not for what I can contribute to the
family's standing.

"Brad, I can't be what you want me to be. We don't
look at life in the same way. My faith, which is the
bedrock of who I am, just isn't as important to you as
your social contacts or your family's importance in the
social and political world. I thought. I wanted." Tears
filled her eyes.

"I thought you would come to Christ and everything
would be all right, even as I tried to change who I am to

suit you. I even cut my hair to please you." She fingered the hair that had begun to grow out again. She'd resisted Mrs. Marsden's hints about getting it cut again.

"What I forgot to do was simply trust Christ? I failed you, Brad. I so wanted...still want...you to commit you life to the Lord, yet I was not trusting Him for my future. I am so sorry."

"Do you understand what you are giving up? As my wife you'd be able to travel throughout the world, meet important political and government figures, be acclaimed as the wife of the heir to Marsden industries..."

Jeanette shook her head. She knew her heart, and it belonged to her Lord--and to John, if he'd have her.

Pulling her close, Brad let her cry against his tan blazer. "I wanted to be sure, Jeanette. No, you have not failed, Darling." A soft smile quirked his lips, "While your methods leave much to be desired, you have not failed."

Her cheeks endearingly damp, Jeanette searched his face. "What, what do you mean?"

"Last night, my little zealot," Brad wiped a tear away with his thumb. "I actually knelt down beside my bed and asked Jesus Christ to come into my life."

His heart lurched at the radiance on Jeanette's face. "Then it's all right! Everything is all right."

Releasing her, Brad smiled sadly, "No, Darling, everything is not all right. You said you do not love me other than as a friend. Tell me honestly." His look booked no hedging, "Do you really want to marry me?"

Closing her eyes against the pain in her heart, Jeanette shook her head. "No, Brad." Then, "You really and truly gave your life to Christ?"

"I really and truly did. Because I did, I understand what you have been trying to tell me all along. I'm sorry I blew up about John." He patted her shoulder, "I have been jealous of John all along, and now I think I know why. You're in love with him, aren't you?"

"How could you know that when I didn't, not until today?"

Kissing her cheek, Brad whispered brokenly, "Go to him Jeanette, and God bless you for bringing me the best gift of all."

"But your mother, the wedding, the gifts..."

"I'll handle that." As he let her out at her house, he told her. "Jeanette, I do love you. If you ever need a friend."

Sniffing, Jeanette leaned over and kissed his cheek. "Oh, Brad, I wish it could have been different."

His chuckle was shaky. "You'd better go Jeanette, while I am still gentleman enough to let you walk out of my life."

Glancing up at the setting sun, Jeanette wondered how she could have been so afraid to admit the truth even to herself. She had hurt Brad, and when they learned about the broken engagement, her parents and his would also be hurt. Most of all, she had failed the Lord. What of John, did he despise her for accepting

Brad? He would know she accepted him for the wrong reasons.

Walking onto the rustic footbridge, Jeanette thought of the first time she and John leaned over the rail and watched the fish flashing in the stream below. Her heart constricted painfully. Yet, joy flooded through her at Brad's commitment to Christ due, she thought, to God's grace, not her own manipulations. Joy mingled with sweet memories of Brad--and John.

Each moment with John she found imprinted in her mind in living color. How she longed to share her heart with him, but suddenly she panicked. What could she say? After being engaged to Brad for a year, how could she tell John how she felt about him? Would he laugh at her?

She could not bear his sarcasm. Clutching the box in her hands, Jeanette stuffed it back into her pocket as she stared through the trees to the evening sky all golden, red and blue. Maybe, John wasn't coming. Had his mother taken a turn for the worst? With a sigh, Jeanette turned to go.

"Jeanette!" Swinging around, Jeanette tripped.

John's arm wrapped about her, holding her so tightly she could scarcely breathe. "Jeanette," he cleared his throat; forced a laugh. "I'm surprised Brad allowed you to come--and alone."

Jeanette swallowed, her cheeks reddened then paled. "We broke up." She showed him her ringless hand.

"Why? I suppose you told him about the letter."

"Of course."

Something about her sobered the grin on his lips. "I'm glad you came."

Jeanette stared down into the clear stream. "It was much more than that. I knew, for a long time. I was so determined to do things my way, I forgot to trust God. I feared facing the truth. I don't love him, John. I don't think I ever did. Not the way I should."

"Is there someone else?" She heard the tone of uncertainty.

Hope welled up inside. "Whom do you suggest?"

A slight smile tugged John's lips. "Was I the reason you lost another ring?"

Growing solemn, he put his hands on Jeanette's shoulders and turned her to face him. She trembled under his touch. "I hurt you Jeanette. I know that."

"And I hurt you."

He stared down into her eyes. "Did you keep the ring?"

Pulling the box from her pocket, Jeanette held it out. Taking it from her, John flicked it open, took out the Blue Sapphire, and slipped it onto her finger. The evening sun caught the stone and reflected its light into her eyes.

Kissing her fingers, he murmured, "My one and only love."

Snatching back her hand, Jeanette blushed. "Stop it! Stop teasing me, John. I can't take it right now." She wrenched away from him, but he forced her to look at him.

"Jeanette, listen. It's not easy for me to admit my feelings. When father left, I felt betrayed. I was afraid to let anyone too close, anyone that is but mother. Not only did father leave, but he left us in such debt, it took mother years to pay it all off. She broke her health, and very young I had to become man of the family.

"I learned to hide my feelings." He growled, "The last year in the marines hasn't changed that."

"John, I must know the truth." Still bruised from her recent breakup, Jeanette had no intention of throwing herself at John. This time she must know for sure.

He glanced away from her. "I joined the marines to forget you. Did you know that? I mean, you'd already chosen Brad. What could I offer in comparison? But," he said, his eyes returned hungrily to her face. "You weren't easy to forget. God put a love for you into my heart, and I didn't know how to get rid of it.

"The truth? When I knew I was coming back because of mother's illness, I decided to see you once more and then forget you--forever. When I was late," he stopped and Jeanette searched his face.

"You're mother, is she?"

"She's going to be fine. She told me about your visits. They meant a lot to her. Thanks."

"That's why you were late?"

"I was afraid I had missed you. Then there you were." He cleared his throat. "Jeanette, I have to be back on duty in two weeks."

"John!" Jeanette wailed.

The pain in her eyes gave him the courage to speak. "I'd like you to return with me...as my wife. It won't be easy being a military wife. At any time, I might be sent off somewhere and not be able to see you for six months, a year. But I want us to make a life together. I want to marry you, Jeanette. Will you marry me?" He hurried on. "Nothing fancy. Your family and mine in our church here. I know that's not what you had planned and what I can offer you is not very much compared to Brad, but...."

Jeanette's mind whirled. "Marry you? Are you sure?"

"Is this too fast, I mean, you just broke up with Brad." The humble plea in his eyes melted her heart.

Throwing her arms about his neck, she confessed. "Oh, John, you don't know how I missed you. I would love getting married in our little church. I always dreamed not of a great big wedding, but a simple service of love. Of course I'll marry you. I'll go anywhere with you!"

"Are you saying," he teased, "you're marrying me for the church?"

"No, because I love you, John Amory. And because it's right."

Chuckling, John swung her around. "And I love you, Jeanette. I love you forever!" His kiss promised a lifetime together bonded with laughter, mutual faith, and love.

This was God's best. This time Jeanette had no doubts.

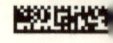

www.ingramcontent.com/pod-product-compliance
Lightning Source LLC